AMETHYST DAWN

ANA MICHELLE

BOOK 2

For Aunt Beth, Grandma Sherri, My sister Kiara, my Mom and my best friend. You all have kept me going on this book and all the rest!

Contents

CHAPTER 1

I WALKED INTO THE kitchen, my arms piled with the dishes from the group dinner and paused. Alec was leaning against the counter next to the slowly brewing coffee maker. His long legs stretched in front of him one tucked over the other at the ankles and his muscled arms were crossed over his chest. His head was tilted back against the cabinets, eyes closed. He was the ideal of my every wet dream since I could remember. Tall, dark, ruggedly handsome, heavily muscled, and a voice that made me want to beg, for anything and everything he would give me.

"See something you like seer?" his deep voice vibrated down my back.

"Maybe," I walked into the kitchen and leaned against the island opposite him. I let my eyes travel down his leanly muscled lower body. My gaze traveled up to his broad chest and arms, before moving to his chiseled jaw and full lips. Finally meeting his laughing chocolate brown eyes with my own blue ones. I let my tongue slide out along my lower lip before continuing, "I would have to see more to know for sure."

"You wouldn't know what to do if you saw more," his lips twitched into a smirk. I almost groaned as I watched his stomach muscles clench when he stood straight from leaning on the counter without uncrossing his arms. He took a step towards me, letting his arms fall to his sides, and then another step. I felt something tighten inside me. I said a curse under my breath and prayed to the Goddess for control and hoped that he wouldn't notice the impact he was having. He leaned towards me and put his hands on the counter on either side of me. When his scent hit me, I gave up all hopes of controlling my erection and instead fought not to press myself against him. "Problem seer?" He whispered suggestively, as his honeyed voice washed over me; I had to close my eyes and swallow. Twice.

"Only problem, Soldier Boy, is that you're still wearing too many clothes."

I whispered back, not sure I could talk any louder in that moment.

He laughed and I felt him move away from me. "One day Zander, I just might take you up on that" he paused, "offer and you won't be saying that," he chuckled, "now why don't you tell me again about these other witches that you guys ran into." I opened my eyes to find his back to me as he poured himself a cup of coffee. The change of topic had me reeling. I shook my head to steady myself.

"If you want that story again you might as well pour me a cup too. Heavy on cream, light on the sugar, sugar," I directed as I made my way over to the small table in the corner and dropped into a chair.

"Watch who you're calling sugar," he grinned over his shoulder at me.

I let my eyes roam over him again and had to appreciate how his jeans hugged him, "oh I'm watching."

He walked over and set a steaming black mug in front of me and I grinned my thanks as he sat down, "so what about these other witches you ran into? Do you know who they were or anything at all about them?" he prompted.

I took a deep breath and sat back in my chair, "there were three of them in the clearing, but I'm pretty sure there are more of them."

"Who were they?" he sat forward, arms resting on the table.

"I don't know. We didn't exactly take the time to interrogate them," I sipped from the mug scowling.

"We need to find out who they are. We could look back into all the covens histories and see what we can find."

"I don't have access to my covens history, but we can talk to the others and see what they have." Before he could answer the doorbell rang. We both looked at each other before standing. Alec gave a short whistle and his familiar a lynx named Croatoan, appeared at his side as we walked into the foyer. Several of the others met us there and we all looked at one another as the bell rang out again. Shaking my head I stepped forward and opened the door.

Standing on the stoop was an Elf. Her skin was the color of moonlight and she had ivory hair that hung straight. Her up tilted eyes were a midnight blue. She wore a zipped black leather jacket and a pair of tight black leather pants with a pair of knee-high boots over them. I could make out the gleam of silver at the tops of her boots and knew she had blades in there.

"Can we help you?" I asked and felt Dazzle, my chameleon familiar, climb from the pocket of my shirt to perch on my shoulder. He pressed the side of his small body against the pulse in my throat.

"I am looking for the Shadow Walker." Her velvet voice wrapped around me and floated into the house.

"I don't know a Shadow Walker," I crossed my arms across my chest.

The Elf gave a sigh of disgust, "the witch from the Shadow Walkers coven. They are here, I can sense their magic. Let me in I can help."

"Let her in Zander. If nothing else we don't need her blabbing on about witches while standing on the stoop," Alec said from next to me.

"Like anyone's gonna bat an eye at someone talking about witches in New Orleans," Eris drawled from where she leaned against the doorway to the parlor.

"What's your name?" Ade asked, Capone growling silently at her heels.

"I will only speak with the Shadow Walker." She said stiffly.

"We already told you we don't know who this Shadow Walker is." Alec growled.

"She means McKenna," Randall said from the stairs. I looked up to see him watching, eyes narrowed, "now who the hell is she?" he nodded his head toward the Elf, who still stood on the porch.

"As I said I will only speak to the Shadow Walker. If you could please tell them I am here, every minute that I stay I am in danger."

"I will go get McKenna," Randall said silently and turned to head back up the stairs.

"Go ahead and let her in," Alec said again from behind me.

I stepped to the side to let the Elf enter, "If you try to harm her, I swear to the universe. Whatever danger you think you are in by being here? It will be nothing compared to the harm that will immediately descend upon you," I said, as she walked past me. My hand fell to finger the vial in my pocket.

"I am not here to harm her, only to help her." She stiffened, glaring at me. We all waited in silence for Randall to return.

It took only a few minutes for him to come back down the stairs, Kenna and Gideon in tow.

"You are the Shadow Walker." The elf said, her eyes on the youngest of us.

"I'm from the Shadow Witch Coven," Kenna said, her voice filled with caution, "Who are you?" she asked. Just then Jamal and Ed came down the stairs to stand behind her and Gideon.

"You have reached the first plane," the Elf stated, stepping forward.

Kenna stepped forward another step, blocking Gideons attempt to come between her and the other woman "But we cannot reach the rest, the gemstones that hold our powers have been stolen. Can you help us?"

"Can we talk some place more private?" the elf asked.

"We are a single team here, anything you tell me they will also hear." Kenna answered quickly.

The Elf took a deep breath and tilted her head back. She let out the breath slowly before looking back at Kenna, "I am ashamed to say that one of my kind joined with the dark witches and took the Gemstones from this plane. She was from another house and felt they needed to be returned to that from which they came. She felt the ability to walk the planes should be that of only the Elves. You should know, not all of us feel that way," she lifted a hand to stop the immediate protest from around the room, "the witches have been manipulating the planes for as long as the Elves. The witches had to solidify their powers into objects instead of keeping the abilities within themselves. We know they did this in order to lessen the likelihood of prosecution during the witch trials, which could have led to you losing the powers, possibly forever. To most of us that does not mean that the witches should lose their rights to the Astral Planes. Elves have never faced that kind of persecution and thus have never had to make that decision. Now, I cannot go to the planes to retrieve your gems, that is not my power. What I can do is magnify your ability and help you reach all seven planes so that you can retrieve the gems."

"What is your name?" Kenna asked again.

"Not here, again not all of my kind agree with me being here, and some will kill me if they find out that it was I who helped you. Now, was there a focus that the gems were placed in?"

"Yes, we have it upstairs." Gideon said.

"Then let us go upstairs."

"And why should we trust you?" Alec asked from next to me.

"Because without an Elf you do not have the ability to reach the planes and retrieve the Gems. Without the

Gems you will never regain your ability to walk the planes." the elf turned to face him, her eyes going cold, "you should trust me because I have nothing to gain by helping you and everything to lose, including my life."

"Kenna, we should discuss this, privately" Randall said softly from where he stood with her on the stairs. She nodded and turned to head into the small living room off the foyer.

"We can keep an eye on our visitor," I said, looking over to Alec who nodded. We stood guard as the others all filed into the small room and closed the door. Every moment they were in the room I had to fight the urge to not eliminate the Elf before she could cause harm to the family we had built here. Gwen came down the stairs a few moments before the others came back into the foyer, but I never took my eyes off the Elf.

"Zander, what's going on?" Kenna asked, coming up to me and setting a hand on my arm.

"Just don't trust her," I whispered.

"Well, we need to trust her," she looked past me to the Elf, "You say you can get us to all seven Astral Planes, how?"

"You already have the natural connection to the Planes; I will just be able to amplify your own abilities. I can only send you to all the Planes Shadow Walker, no one else here has the ability to reach the first Plane unassisted."

"She isn't going anywhere with you alone." Gideon said, and it already sounded like an old argument.

"Gideon," Kenna's voice was exasperated.

"I will agree to allow five in the room with us. Four to uphold the elements, and one to place the gems onto the focus as they return to this plane. However, I do not have the ability to send anyone but the Shadow Walker into the Astral Planes, I myself do not even have the ability to travel there with her." she said, looking between Gideon and Kenna.

"Five will be more than enough," Kenna said before any of us could object.

"Then please choose your protectors and let us move to where you have the focus so that we may get things moving."

"Gideon, Randall, Zander, Ade," Kenna looked between Alec and Gwen, before turning to Gideon.

"Alec," he nodded towards the former Marine next to me, "and Gwen will be just outside the room with her healing kit in case something goes awry."

"I will agree to that." the Elf nodded.

"Ed, Jamal, Eris, why don't you guys activate the protection wards around the property? I have a feeling that whatever we are about to do could use the extra security," Alec said.

"We can do that." Ed said with a nod. He led the others out the front door and Gwen headed upstairs to the small room that she had rela-beled the infirmary. Randall turned and led the way up the stairs with the rest of us following closely behind, the Elf in the middle.

Once we were all inside the attic Kenna turned back to the Elf, "What is your name, please? I don't want to keep calling you, Elf."

"You can call me Morgana," she said.

Chapter 2

ALEC, RANDALL, ADE AND myself all stood in front tall single candle holders that someone had procured from an abandoned church. Each one of us had a large pillar candle of a different color atop the holder. "We need you to chant in time with the others. You can not stop until either the Shadow Walker wakes or the last Gem appears," The elf directed from the center of the room where she had moved after positioning us around the circle. She stood near the Altar, as if drawn to the faint magic it had "I have given you each a piece of paper. Use the words on them to call upon the Elven Directions."

"As if we don't all use the same four corners," Alex grumbled under his breath earning a glare from the Elf.

Kenna and Gideon separated from where they stood off to the side and walked to the pile of blankets we arrangd made for her. Kenna laid down and Morgana knelt next to her, her hands hovering over Kenna's temples.

I looked across the circle at Alec as we lit the candles in front of us. He met my eyes and I lifted a brow in question, Kenna had become like a little sister to me and I had never seen him work magic. He gave one short nod and I let out a small sigh of relief. I nodded back and closed my eyes. I let my magic fill me, before it flowed from my hands. I cupped my hands around the flame of the blue candle, close enough to feel the heat on my palms. Taking a deep breath I began the chant I had already memorized. I repeated the words, hearing my voice meld and mix with the other three. With each word I could feel the magic rise and pulse around me.

I lost count of how many times I said the words, each time I could feel myself begin to weaken. I lifted my gaze from the flickering flame of the candle and met Alec's dark brown eyes. I took a deep breath between words and felt my magic center me and grow. I saw Kenna's body buck and writhe on the ground before growing still and I felt my heart clench. There was no way that she was coming out of this whole, if she came out of this at all. The magic pulsed as Gideon rose and paced the circle. I could hear his voice and Morgana's but their words were muffled to my ears, the four chants filling my senses. I kept my eyes locked on Alec's. I didn't know how much longer I could keep doing this, I could feel my energy draining with every word I whispered. I saw Gideon scramble towards the altar and the Elf step up behind him. She spoke to him in a hushed voice and he raised his hands over the surface. His body slumped forward over the table and with a glance backward the Elf walked out from the circle. When she pushed through the ring of magic it felt like something sliced across me. I stumbled over the words and watched the flame flicker on the candle. Quickly I righted myself and pulled on the reserve of power inside me.

"My job is done here, I have done all I can." She said to all of us and none of us before she left the attic. After what seemed like an eternity Gideon went rigid again and his fists slammed on the altar.

"Where's Kenna?" Ade asked, stopping her chant and I felt my heart clench. I stopped my spell. We had failed.

"Where is she?" Gideon growled looking up at us. I stumbled back to lean against the wall exhausted and watched the flame of the candle flicker out as I slid down to sit.

"She left as soon as you slipped into the astral plane, she said her job here was finished." Alec said as he knelt next to me and held out a Gatorade.

"She knew," I whispered looking up at the others, "She knew as soon as Kenna didn't wake up and she didn't want to be here to face you."

"Get Gwen," Gideon said, turning to Randall. I felt the ache in my chest grow at pain and desperation in his voice. "I need her, now." Randall turned and left. I started to push myself off the floor but there was a heavy hand on my shoulder stopping me.

I looked up and met Alec's concerned eyes, "stay sitting and drink. You need to replenish yourself, we all do. That spell took it out of all of us." I looked to the left and saw Ade in a similar position to me against the wall under the small window.

I nodded in her direction, "let me go over by Ade and I'll rest," I whispered. I stood and made my way over to the young girl with Alec hovering near me. I slid down next to her and bumped my shoulder into hers, "you ok?" I whispered as Randall and Gwen came back into the room. We watched Gideon take Gwen by the hand. He led her over to the Altar, whispering with urgency whatever words the Elf had given him.

Ade looked up at me and I noticed she had tear tracks running down her cheeks, "I liked her you know. Sure, she was all rays of sunshine and Ms. Got to do the right thing, but I liked her." She whispered. I slid my arm over her shoulders and pulled her against my side as Alec sat down next to me on the other side.

"We all liked her," I said, leaning my head against hers, "those of us who had gotten to know her at least." I watched as Gwen and Gideon came back to us. Gwen walked over to stand next to Randall who was leaning heavily against the wall. We all watched as Gideon lifted Kenna's still form into his arms, cradling her against his chest.

As he left the room Randall called his name, only to be silenced by Gwen's hand on his arm. "Leave him alone to grieve his love," she said, her soft voice and blue eyes filled with grief. I leaned a little into Alec, still holding Ade to me, as I sipped at the over sugared drink he had given me.

I flinched when I heard the door one floor down close. We all sat there for a minute in silence. Gwen slipped an arm around Randall when he started toward the door, her slender frame the only thing that hid his fatigued gate.

"I think I'm going to go lay down for a bit," Ade said softly as she stood, Capone pressing himself to her side. She reached a hand down to rest on his head as she left the room.

"We should go tell the others," I said looking at Alec.

He nodded and stood offering me a hand. As I stood I felt Dazzle climb from my pocket and press himself around my neck. Instantly I felt a spark of energy course through me. Looking over I saw Croatoan pressed to the side of Alec's leg and I could see him growing stronger by the second. We made our way down the stairs to where the others waited.

"Well," Eris asked pausing in her pacing of the front parlor, "did she get the Gems back? Can we walk the astral planes again?"

"She did get the garnets back, but she didn't survive," I glared at the annoying up tight blonde. Misty and Esme sunk back into their seats covering their mouths, Jamal and Ed swore looking down.

Alec put a calming hand on my back, "the Astral Portals will need to be re-solidified but we do have the ability to Astral Project safely."

Gwen walked in and handed both Alec and ME a glass filled with a thick creamy liquid. I looked down at the cup and the at the older witch quirking an eye brow. "It's a protein smoothy. Drink it" she ordered in her normal calm and no nonsense voice. "What ever spell that woman had you doing seems to have drained each of you considerably and now is not the time for any of us to be weak."

I saw Eris's face fill with something that looked like worry in her eyes at Gwen's words and rushed from the room and up the stairs. Taking a deep breath I drank the contents of the glass down in a few large gulps, surprised to find that it didn't taste as bad as expected. I smiled a little when I saw a look of shock in Alec's eyes as he finished his own drink. He took the now empty glass from my hand and headed toward the kitchen without a word.

"I'll be in my room." I shook my head and walked out, heart heavy with loss. The climb up the stairs was slow. Gwen was right, I was completely drained, even with Dazzles small body pressed against my neck. As I crested the first landing I saw Eris rush into her and Ade's room, a glass in hand with what seemed to be the same smoothy shake thing Gwen had given me down stairs. Maybe the ice queen wasn't as cold as we all thought. I turned into my room and set Dazzle down on the night stand before falling face first onto the mat-tress. Even before my head hit the pillow I felt sleep close around me.

CHAPTER 3

I WOKE UP A few hours later, feeling slightly better but still tired. Leaning over I ran a finger along Dazzles back as he snoozed under the heat lamp and felt a thrill of power run up my arm. Letting the small rush disperse through my body I stood with a stretch and moved over to grab my deck of cards from the top of the dresser. Sitting back on the small bed, legs crossed and back against the wall, I shuffled the well-worn deck of Tarot Cards. The paper was smooth and going thin in spots. It was my favorite deck, and was the standard Ryder Wayde deck my mother had given me when I was ten and first showing interest. Even though I had grown my collections of decks to nearly triple digits, this was still my go to and the only one I had brought with me. Closing my eyes I flipped the top three cards over in the easy past, present, future spread. Opening my eyes I swore. I scooped the cards up and shuffled them back into the deck. This time I pulled the top ten cards, positioning them into the standard Celtic cross spread.

"Son of a bitch," I growled and pulled the cards back into my hand. Shuffling again I racked my brain for another spread. I turned the top five cards and laid them into the Success spread. I had done this same layout for so many people during my beginning days on the Vegas strip. With a frustrated sigh I scooped the cards back up and put them back into the black velvet pouch. I stood from the bed and walked to my dresser. I set the pouch back onto the cherry wood top and grabbed one of the other small draw string velvet bags that I had placed up there. The bag rattled as I lifted it and made my way back to my bed.

"Are you expecting those to tell you something different?" Alec's voice startled me from my concentration.

I looked up at him as I sat on the edge of the bed, "Am hoping they will." I murmured looking down at the bag of runes.

"What is it telling you that you don't like?"

"You wouldn't understand even if I told you," I looked up at him.

He walked in and sat in the small chair in the corner, "Try me. I tend to understand more than people give me credit for."

"Every reading I do, with every lay-out for the tarot cards, keeps telling me I need to go back home."

"And that's a bad thing?"

"There is nothing left for me back there." I scowled and clenched my fist around the soft velvet bag. I could feel the hard runes pressing into my palm through the soft fabric, "there hasn't been anything for me there since I was fourteen. Not since my mother died."

"I'm sorry," his voice was soft. When I looked up he was looking up at me and his eyes showed sorrow.

"Thank you. Would you like to see her?" I asked without thinking, shock-ing myself. I hadn't thought about her in years.

"I would," his smile was soft. I walked back to the dresser, placing the pouch down and opened the top drawer. I slipped my hand under the pile of folded t-shirts and pulled out the small frame that I kept wrapped in a thin, blue silk scarf. I unwrapped the frame as I walked over to him, tucking the scarf in my back pocket. The scarf had been hers, but had lost even the faintest of her scent years ago. The frame was silver that was starting to tarnish in places. It was small, a little bigger than the palm of my hand, and ornate. The picture inside was of a young woman in her mid-twenties. She had long black hair with cobalt blue eyes that sparkled with joy. I handed him the frame and he took it gently in his hands. I leaned against the wall and crossed my arms watching him.

He looked at the photo as if he were trying to memorize it, then he looked up at me, "She's beautiful. You look just like her." He extended the framed photo back to me and I took it gazing down at her.

"Thank you. I never could figure out if that was the reason my father hated me or if it truly was the fact that I was gay." I sighed and walked over to put the picture on the nightstand next to my bed, like she had resided back home.

"You and your father don't get along I take it?" Alec asked. His voice wasn't judgmental or prying, but neutral, as if he were asking what color the sky way.

I shook my head with a laugh, "Nope. He wanted a son, I just wasn't the son he wanted. I was too feminine in his mind. I didn't like sports but instead preferred the theatre. The outdoors held no appeal for me, I would instead opt to stay inside with my mother. To this day I have the thought of getting dirty, but I can sew like no ones business. I like boys, not girls," I laughed, but it was hollow, "he could have forgiven the rest if it hadn't been for that last one. That was an interesting day at the dinner table. I think if my mother hadn't been alive when I came out, he would have disowned me right then and there, and that was if he didn't just kill me out right. I still think the only reason he let me stay after she died was because of a promise he made to her. The day I turned eighteen though? He woke me up at five am and told me I had until he got home from work to get the hell out. No one in the coven stopped him either. Not that they had stopped him when he was throwing me into walls or smacking me around while drunk. So, I packed up a duffle bag and a suitcase and I headed to Vegas." I looked up at Alec and could see the anger in his eyes, "That was the last day I saw anyone from my coven, well mostly. My older sister cried when I left, hugged me tight as she could, but she was afraid of him by then. It took her a decade before she reached out and we met for dinner. She is the only one I miss. We meet up about twice a year for breakfast or lunch, though we had to skip the last few as she had running to do for our father. Any more than that and the old bastard would get suspicious."

"How did you make it on your own?"

"Well like I said I went to Vegas, specifically the strip. When I got there I took some of the cash that I had been hiding away and went to a small printing company and had them make me some business cards. I became a street corner clairvoyant. I bought a suite and played up my flamboyancy and people loved it. The first week I made enough to start a bank account. By the end of the first month I had enough for a small studio apartment." I grinned at him, "my dad called me six months later and said that I was abusing my powers. He told me that the coven was furious with me, said I had to stop immediately. So I started practicing some of the other powers we had and shifted from predicting people's futures to performing as a street magician. It wasn't as lucrative and gave me one hell of a head ache most nights, but it still paid the bills. Then last month I woke up to my sister calling me, telling me that the magic wasn't working. Sure enough, when I went out that night I couldn't perform my normal tricks. When I got home, I had a dream that was pre-monition, and I called my sister and she spoke to our high priestess. When she called back she told me that they needed to me to go to Salem, Mass-achusetts. She told me that if I could get the powers working again then the high priestess would allow me to go back to telling the people in the streets what slot machine to use."

"Wow, the Circle seems like great people." He grimaced.

I laughed at his dry tone until my stomach hurt and tears were leaking from my eyes. I clutched my sides, leaning against the wall, and still I laughed. When I could finally catch my breath I looked at him, hands braced on my knees, and the grin on his face had me laughing again, "yeah, they are the best." I wheezed out when I could finally form words, and wiped the tears from my eyes.

He stood still smiling and shook his head, "Its late and we have all had a long day. I'm going to head to bed, but I think you should think on what the cards are telling you, instead of hoping that you can get another answer from somewhere else." He left the room and I fell back onto my bed.

I looked over at the small terrarium I had made for Dazzle on the night stand, "Let's hope tomorrow things get better." I turned off the lamp and rolled over, drifting into an exhausted sleep.

Chapter 4

I walked through a dark pathway, my foot steps echoing on the stone floor. The silver moonlight streaming through the windows casting shadows and highlighting faces frozen in stone. Ever time I turned away from one face twisted in agony I came face-to-face with another of the. My pulse raced and I rushed past one after another, needing to escape the maze that they formed. Looking over my shoulder at statues and felt myself hit something cold and smooth. I pushed back stumbling and found myself standing outside a glass crypt. Through the glass I could see two cloth draped bodies lying on raised platforms. I scrambled back away from the tomb and tripped falling backwards. I landed in water and tried to scramble back to my feet when a wave washed over me. I tumbled in the water, the world swirling and blurring around me. The water washed away, and I laid on the cold cement, choking up the water that had found its way into my burning lungs. I blinked as neon lights spun around me until the "Welcome to Vegas" sign stabilized in front of me. The bright lights of the sign blinding me to the world around me.

I jerked up choking. My throat and nose burned as water flowed down my chin and drenched my chest. I scrambled from the bed and turned my light on. Grabbing a towel, I mopped the water from my skin and pulled a t-shirt on. and walked over to the open terrarium where Dazzle was. I ran my finger over Dazzle before lifting him and curling him into my pocket. I stepped into my hard bottomed slippers and walked out into the dark hall. The shadows cast from the slivers of moonlight gave me flashes back to the dream. I made my way through the silent house and down the stairs into the back garden. The fresh air soothed the burn from the water and for a moment I stood and just breath in the air.

Eventually I made my way through the raised garden beds Ed had been building, there was wood stacked to the side still for the rest of the beds he still had to build. They were still empty but the girls had been making plans over dinner the night before about what to fill them with. I walked across the pavement and leaned against the fence looking out over the street. I closed my eyes and listened to the murmur of people a few streets over. I breathed deep, the smell of New Orleans floating through me as the sounds of the quarter faintly echoed down the empty streets, and I ached for home.

I missed the lights and sounds of Vegas. The flash of neon so bright making it seem like it's always day-time. The ringing of slot machines, the shouts of laughter and triumph. So many voices they blended and blurred into one, and yet if you listen close enough you could almost separate them. The smell of so many different foods floating in the air, that choose what to eat was never an easy option.

"You ok?" Alec's deep soft voice shocked me from my memories and back to the present.

"Yeah, had another dream, woke up choking up water." I answered softly not looking at him.

"Are you ok?" he asked again, his voice thick with real concern this time.

I nodded twice before letting my head hang down, "Its not the first dream I have had bleed into the real world. Though it's only the second since we lost the ability of premonition and the most confusing I have ever had."

"Tell me about the dream," he leaned against the fence next to me.

"It was dark, there were strange statues of people in angony. Then there was a glass building with two bodies inside. I stumbled back away from it and fell into water. Waves rushing over me before depositing me onto the Las Vegas strip looking up at the welcome sign." I finally looked up at him.

"I can't help with most of it, never was good with any type of precognition, but I think we both can agree to what the ending means."

"I have to go back home, to the Seers Circle." I agreed, "The same things that the cards told me earlier."

"You won't be going alone you know." His voice was soft. I nodded and turn my back to the fence tilting my head back to look up at dark sky, the clouds covering the remaining sliver of the waning moon.. I felt him turn and slip an arm over my shoulders pulling me against him, "You won't face him alone." He whispered as I let my head fall against his shoulder, let myself sink into the warmth of his body. I closed my eyes when he tilted his head to rest on mine and let myself forget for a little bit longer about the hell I would be walking into soon.

We stayed like that until we both started to doze off while standing. A silent agreement had us moving back into the house and we walked up to the bedrooms. Alec squeezed my hand at my doorway and I walked back inside falling back onto the bed. Dazzle crawled from my shirt pocket and curled against my neck just above my shoulder. I closed my eyes and willed myself back to sleep, hoping this time it would be a dreamless sleep.

I opened my eyes to the sky slowly brightening outside the window. I sighed, feeling dread settle over me. Rolling from bed, Dazzle still snoozing on the pillow, I made my way to the small closet. It was time to pack for the trip back home. I pulled the small duffle from the closet and set it on the bed. I grabbed the half a dozen or so velvet bags from the dresser and put them into the duffle. I pulled the silk scarf from the back of my jeans from the day before and grabbed the small photo frame from the nightstand. I pressed my finger to my mothers face before wrapping the picture and tucking it into the bag. Since I was going back home I only added two outfits to get me through the drive there.

Prodding Dazzle awake I lifted him to my shoulder and grabbed the bag before walking down the stairs. I found the rest of the group, minus Gideon, around the table all looking sadly at their mostly full breakfast plates. I set my bag down in the hall-way and walked in.

Taking a deep breath I addressed them all, "I'm going to look for the Amethyst Mirror and to see if I can learn anything about the witches who took the artifacts." I said calmly, meeting Alec's eyes.

CHAPTER 5

"DO YOU WANT ANY leads on where it could be?" Ade asked her hand dropping to Capone's head in what I had learned was a nervous gesture.

"Everything points to me needing to go back to Vegas and talking with my old coven." I felt a fine tremor run up my spine at the thought and pushed down the feeling of dread.

"You aren't going alone," Ed said scooting back his chair.

"He's right. From what you all told us about the other witches hints to them being powerful and dangerous." Randall said from the head of the table, "None of us should be going anywhere alone until we figure out who they are."

"Any who want to come are welcome. I'm leaving within the hour." I nodded once and walked out of the dining room. I made my way up the stairs to the door to the room where Kenna was. I pressed my palm to the door and felt a new wave of sorrow wash over me. I stood back and lifted my hands. I closed my eyes and took a deep breath. I traced my hands in the air in front of the door. Moving them in the patterns of the runes for life and death, connecting them with the rune for healing. I pushed as much power I could into the figures, hopefully locking whatever life was left in Kenna to this world, to keep her here until we could find a way to get her back. Dropping my hands back to my sides I headed back downstairs, knowing that that was the best I could do for her at this time. I grabbed my bag and headed outside to wait for the others. I sat on the front porch steps and leaned back looking up at the overcast sky above. I'm not sure how long I sat looking up at the clouds before Alec, Ed, and Randall all walked out. They each had bags similar to my own slung over their shoulders.

"So tell us how you know that you need to go back home," Randall said, stopping to lean against the railing of the stairs, his arms crossed over his chest.

"After yesterday I pulled my Tarot cards out and did a few Spreads. There were three cards that kept showing up no matter how many times I pulled. The cards were the Eight of Wands, the Five of Wands, and Judgement, for me these all are indicative of going home. When I went to bed last night I had a dream, it had strange statues, a glass building, water, and the Welcome to Vegas sign. I wouldn't take a normal dream seriously but when I woke up I was choking and coughing up water." I looked up at Ed and Randall, "These dreams are about as close as I get to premonitions since our powers have stopped working."

"Do you think that the Amethyst Mirror is in Vegas?" Ed asked, brow wrinkled in thought.

"It's possible, but I doubt it." I pushed myself to my feet with a sigh. "Who knows maybe we will find a clue about where it is. Whatever the case is, something or someone wants me to go back home. Maybe someone in the coven can tell us about the witches that took the artifacts." I paced, my hand running through my hair, "I have no idea what we will find when we get there."

"Do you think that it will help us to get Kenna back?" Randall asked looking up at the small window of the room where Kenna was.

"The mirror? No," I shook my head, "Not directly. But we can use the mirror to find the other artifacts. Once we have them, I think we can use them to get her back though."

"Care to share how?" Ed asked.

"Not yet, I need to learn a little more about each artifact, and then maybe I can figure something out." I looked at the other three, "We ready to go?"

They all nodded, "One question," Randall said, "how are we getting there with a wolf, a lynx, and a cougar in tow? Not to mention the four of us and our bags"

"Good question," I laughed and shook my head, "Guess we need to find a vehicle for all of us."

After a quick search, we found someone local selling a cargo van with two rows of seats. We had a quick meeting with the others and decided it was a good investment for the lot of us, so Randall and Ed headed over to buy it. When they got back we loaded our bags into the back before standing back and letting the three large familiars jumped in and lay down, huddled together like old friends.

Randall and Ed got into the front while I settled in the back with Alec. I pulled my cell phone from my pocket and sent my sister a text, "I'm coming home." I turned the phone off and tucked it into my bag and pulled out a pen and notebook.

I made a list of the powers we had lost down the left side. Next to each, I wrote the name of the coven best known for use of that power. I drew a line between the two and another line on the other side of the coven names, a few of the powers remaining blank. Next to the Shadow Walk coven, I wrote down McKenna's Name and then the Garnet Altar. Repeating the pattern, I put my name down after the Seers circle and I wrote down the Amethyst Mirror after my name.

"How far is the drive?" Ed asked as he scanned over the old fashioned map he had grabbed.

"If we didn't make a single stop almost exact twenty four hours." I answered absently not looking up from the page.

"I'm thinking we should do just that," He answered, "I'm not thinking its gonna be easy to find a hotel willing to take in the three in the back."

"We could probably break it into four six hour rotations for driving," Randall suggested from the driver seat."

"We can stop for dinner and swap then." Alec added in.

"Alec, what coven are you from?" I asked softly looking at the list, interrupting their planning.

"The People of Roanoke, why?" he glanced over at me from where he was sitting.

"What are you looking for?" I asked scanning over the list and writing his name next to the correct coven. I looked up at him and lifted an eyebrow, "energy fields huh?"

"Yeah, they were really helpful when I was overseas." He slid closer and looked over the list I was working on, "that's a great idea." He said eyes scanning.

I nudged him, "glad you think so. Want to tell me what we are looking for?"

"Oh right, the Energy Fields come from a Citrine Gazing Ball." I added the info to the page.

"Ed what about you?" I asked

"From the Big Sky Coven, was sent to look for the Ruby Offering bowl so we can talk to all our ancestors again." His answer was unsurprisingly short and concise. I added the information as he said it.

"Randall?" I had noticed the older man's shoulders stiffening as we had all talked.

"South Dakota was home to the Badland Brotherhood." His voice was just above a whisper.

"I haven't heard of them," Ed said turning to look at our driver.

"There's not many of us left," his voice was soft. "About fifteen years ago someone or something came through and killed most of us. We were known for teleportation. I was going through some old Grimoires when the magic stopped. I found out that all of our powers came from these artifacts. Teleportation, in particular, came from a wand made with aquamarine." I was staring at him, still processing that an entire coven had been wiped out and no one knew about it. Alec nudged me and I quickly added the coven, Randall's name, and the wand to the list.

We settled into silence and I looked over the list again. I added Gwen's name by healing next to the Serenity Circle. At the bottom of the page, I wrote the other names. I leaned against the window and let my eyes close and thought over what each of the others could be looking for.

I must have fallen asleep as I woke up when Randall stopped at a drive-through. We decided to order two dozen cheeseburgers and Tyr gave a yip of agreement from the back. After the teenager brought out the four paper sacks we drove until we found an empty parking lot about ten minutes down the road near what seemed to be a park. We let the three familiars out from the back and let them stretch their legs. I munched happily on my burgers as I leaned back against the van and watched the others tossing sandwiches into the air for their familiars to run after and catch. By the time we got back into the van, Ed taking the driver seat this time, the familiars were panting as they jumped into the back. I settled back against the window and closed my eyes again, knowing that after the next stop it would be mine and Alec's turn up front.

Chapter 6

I PULLED OFF THE interstate and the sights of home greeted me. I steered away from the main strip and stopped at the curb outside the apartment building I had lived at for half of my life now.

"Where are we?" Ed asked with a sleepy yawn as I powered off the van.

"My apartment. We can clean up here and I'll make a few calls. Hopefully I can get someone from the coven to agree to meet us, otherwise I'll just muscle my way in." I pulled my keys from my backpack and opened the bottom door, I held it open while the others walked in with their familiars by their side, "Top floor all the way down." I informed as I stepped in behind them. I followed the parade up the six flights of stairs and slipped passed them down the hallway. I opened the door and again held the door while they piled in, "Its not much but its home." I said dropping my backpack on the table and lifting Dazzle to one of the millions of vines that traced every inch of the apartment.

"You pay for this on a street magician's salary?" Alec said as he walked the room.

I shrugged and turned away, "I may have used my premonitions a time or two at the casinos when I fell on hard times."

"Good thing our powers don't care about personal gain," Ed laughed.

I laughed and nodded, "If they did I would be on the streets. I'm going to go make a few calls, make yourselves at home." I walked to my room and flipped the light on closing the door. I pulled out my phone and turned it back on. Ignoring the barrage of texts from my sister I called her. She answered on the first ring.

"Zander? Are you ok? What's going on? No one has been able to get any powers to work other than getting the Astral Planes Portals back up and running."

"Take a deep breath Katia," I sat on the edge of my bed and shook my head laughing softly, "I'm ok. I need to talk to the Priestess. I was laying

Tarot cards and had another dream last night, both pointed at me needing to come home. Can you set up a meeting with her?"

"I'll call her," her voice was hesitant, "but it may not be her that you need to talk to."

"I know, I am probably going to need to talk to dad while I am here." I fell back on the bed barely suppressing a groan.

"Yes, but that's still not who I meant. You need to call Lana."

I sat up suddenly at the mention of the first friend I had made after leaving home, "What about Lana?"

"Just call her Z," my sister voice went soft, "I have a feeling she will be of more help than anyone in the coven." With those last words she hung up the phone. I looked down at my phone for a long moment before I scrolled through my contacts until I found Lana's number. Tapping on it I called my old friend wondering if she would be up yet.

"Hello?" her sleepy voice brought back so many memories that I smiled.

"It's been too long Lana."

"Zander," I could hear the smile in her voice past the sleep, "it's been way too long my friend. I heard about what's happening with the witches, is that why you are calling?"

"I'm back home after some travel-ing Lana, and when I called Katia with some questions she suggested I call you."

"She didn't tell you?" Her voice was clear now.

"No. I called to say that I needed to talk to the coven about a few ques-tions I had, and she suggested that I call you.

Lana laughed lightly, "we have a lot of catching up to do my friend, and I think its best we do this in person. Can you meet me and Katia at The Four Corners casino?"

I felt my brow wrinkle, "The Four Corners? There is no such place."

She laughed, "there is now. Come find us there and I will get you fully caught up to everything going on here in Vegas since you left a month ago, and I'll bring all your mail."

"I was wondering why my mailbox wasn't overflowing," I chuckled.

"I'll always have your back." We set-tled on meeting just after sundown, said our goodbyes and hung up. I quickly looked up The Four Corners Casino and saw it was a tiny new casi-no about five miles off the strip. Tuck-ing my phone into my pocket I headed back out to the living room. The guys were lounging on my slightly worn black leather couches, eyes trained to the TV.

"We have a meeting around six at a casino with a few people who may have information for us." I said leaning against a wall, arms crossing over my chest.

"I thought you were going to set up a meeting with your coven, isn't that what your dream told you to do?" Randall asked looking over at me.

I shook my head, "All I got from the premonition was that I needed to come home. I called my sister, the only real link I have to the coven anymore, and she suggested that the coven may not be the reason I needed to come here. So I called a friend at my sisters insistence and she requested we join her after sundown."

"Why can't we meet her now? Do we really have time to waste?" Ed asked concern filling his voice.

"She's a Vampire, can't come out before dark." I said and met each of their eyes my own filled with challenge.

"You trust her?" Alec asked when my eyes met his.

"More than I trust the coven." I answered with a shrug, "Lana was the only person I had for a long time."

"Ok, then we will meet with her and see what she has to say." He nodded.

"Well, what are we going to do for the next eight-ish hours?" Randy asked.

"We could go get food, I don't have anything here and your guys will need meat."

"so, grocery shopping?" Ed asked.

"After we stop for food for us," I laughed.

An hour later we were all walking down the strip. I led them to one of my favorite restaurants, and after slipping the girl at the front a twenty and wink, we were sat at a small booth in the back. We each picked up a menu scanning it for a few minutes.

"How do you stand all the hustle and bustle of this place?" Ed asked from across from me.

"I love it," I laughed. "The lights and night life, it's a town that never sleeps. Vegas isn't just a place, it's a thing. It almost breathes with life itself. Living here, you don't ever have to question if you are alive or not, the city lets you know that you are."

Just then the waiter came over and we each placed our orders. The small talk continued until our meals came and we all ate in silence. As we walked out, I realized Alec hadn't said much of anything since we had gotten to the restaurant.

"Hey everything ok?" I ask quietly bumping my shoulder into his.

"Fine."

"What's going on?" I said stepping in front of him, blocking his path and letting the others increase the space in front of us.

"Do you flirt with everyone?"

"What?"

"Nothing, forget it, we have to much to do." Alec stepped around me and extended his pace to catch up with Randall and Ed. Shaking my head and cursing under my breath I jogged to cut him off.

"Its obviously not nothing," I said stopping in front of him again, "Tell me what's bothering you."

He looked away, his jaw clenched. I watched him force himself to calm but didn't understand what had him so upset to begin with, "You winked at the hostess when you slipped her the twenty for us to jump the wait list. You have flirted with nearly every person we have spoken to since leaving New Orleans. Its stupid but when you were all flirty with me back at the house I thought it was because you actually liked me and now I'm realizing that I was stupid and you just flirt with everyone."

"I don't flirt with everyone." I corrected him, " I may be a little more friendly here but I learned long ago that's how you up your tips." I shrugged, "I guess being back home has pushed me back into some old habits. I didn't do any of it to hurt you." I reached out and laid my hand on his arm, feeling him stiffen under my touch, "And I do like you." I tried to ignore the blush that I felt creeping up my neck, "I like you a whole lot. I will try to tone it down for you but if it starts getting to be too much for you just tell me to tone it down ok?"

I felt the deep breath he took before he relaxed, "Yeah I can do that."

CHAPTER 7

WE STOPPED OUTSIDE ONE of the smallest casinos I had ever seen in Vegas. It stood four stories of old brick and seemed to have a neon sign in every warehouse style window. I started to walk towards the front door with the overly large security guard standing next to it when I heard my name being called softly from the side of the building. I looked and saw my sister peaking around the corner and waving us over. With a silent tilt of my head I lead the others toward the side where she had ducked back into the shadows.

"I was expecting that you guys would have your familiars with, so I've been watching for you." She said as we approached. My sister stood about a head shorter than me, around five foot five. She had cut her blue-black hair into a short bob since the last time I saw her and had it tucked back behind her ears. As usual her face was clean of any makeup. She was wearing a pair of faded jeans and a plain light blue T-shirt.

"We thought walking down the strip with a cougar, a lynx, and a wolf would be a little suspicious." I grinned pulling her into a hug. It had been over a year since we had seen each other, and I held on tight. "How have you been?" I whispered into her hair, not yet ready to let her go.

"Things have become more tense since the powers stopped working. Everyone is on edge." She said, stepping back to look up at me. "Have you guys found anything yet?"

"We are working on it Katia. That's why we are here," I gestured to the others with a nod of my head, "It's why we need help. Do you remember the story that Merlyn used to tell the coven children? The one about the Guardians and the artifacts, where the powers had been locked away?"

"Of course, it was our favorite." She smiled, "She still tells that story to the littles around Yule."

"It was all true Katia, but I think there are parts of that story missing. Let's get inside and I will tell you and Lana everything at once, not to mention I don't think this is something we need regular people over hearing and telling their friends about." I waved the other three over from where they had stopped to give us the privacy to catch up with each other without them as an audience. When they got there, I introduced them to my sister. "Katia this is Randall from the Badland Brotherhood, Ed from the Big Sky Coven, and this is Alec. He's from The People of Roanoke." She shook each of their hands before leading us along the side of the building to a metal door that she held open for us, kicking aside the rock she had used to prop the door open. Inside there was only one place to go once inside the door and that was up a set of cement stairs.

"All the way up," Katia instructed as the door closed behind her and she started up the steps.

"What is it with you two and not using elevators?" Randall grouched, following her up.

"Healthier." We said at the same time from either end of the group. We looked at one another across the others and laughed as our eyes met. For a moment I felt like I was truly home again. I could hear a few grumbles in front of me and couldn't help but grin. When I got to the top landing

Lana was leaning against a dark metal door, her arms crossed behind her back, and she was smiling. Her dark brown hair was braided and hung over her shoulder and her blue eyes twinkled when she looked at me.

"Lana Loo!" I grinned running over and wrapped my arms around her and lifted her off her feet spinning her around.

"Put me down you barbarian!" she laughed, hugging me back as she did.

"I am not the barbarian between the two of us," I smirked at the joke between us, setting her on her feet. I kept my arm around her shoulder as we turned to face the others, "Lana Loo, this is Randall, Ed, and Alec." I said introducing her to the three of them.

"He's hot." she whispered and smirked up at me.

"Shut up," I said through gritted teeth as I grinned back at her knowing she would now demand an explanation.

"So, what is going on, why did you come back to Vegas before you got the mirror back?" Katia asked as she leaned against one of the other walls.

I took a deep breath to begin telling them the story, "I went to Salem like we talked about," I said. I slid down to sit on the floor and leaning against the wall, the others all following my lead, accept Randal who muttered about old knees. "I found the clearing, but the guardians were dead. They had all been slaughtered, and left on the ground where they had dropped." I let my head fall back against the wall, eyes closing as I remembered that day, "My guess is it happened the same day that the powers stopped. The Amethyst Mirror, along with the other artifacts had been stolen, not a single trace of them had been left for us to follow. Someone who witnessed the last murder stepped forward and offered to help. We buried the guardians and then went with the witness. We found three witches that didn't belong to any of the twelve covens and they had the Garnet Altar which is what gave us the Astral Planes. We got it back from them but they had removed the gems so it didn't work. Two days ago, a brave young witch gave her life to retrieve the gems. It's why the covens can walk the Astral Planes again. Starting that night though I started getting signs, signs that pointed me back here." I opened my eyes and looked at my sister, knowing she would be the only person here who could truly understand," The last was a dream that ended with me here in Vegas before

I woke up coughing up water. After that," I nodded to where Alec leaned against the stair railing arms crossed over his broad chest, "Alec convinced me to come back. To reach out to the Coven." I watched Katia's eyes as I finished, "and to Dad."

"You can meet with Marilyn without Dad there," Katia's voice was barely above a whisper.

"No," I shook my head, "I wont hide from him while I am here."

"Were there any clues as to where they took the artifacts?" Lana asked pensively.

"The only thing we had was the witness and he could only take us to the Altar, to the last people to leave the clearing." I said shaking my head, "I'm hoping that once we get the mirror, we can use that to find the other artifacts. We need to get the other artifacts back and to restore all the powers to the witches." I looked at the other three and hesitated before voicing the last, "and maybe then we can bring back the girl who gave her life."

"How are you going to do that?" Lana asked.

"We don't know. What we do know though is if we want to have any chance of doing so we need all of the artifacts back and in place."

"You have nothing to help us find the artifacts?" Katia asked.

"The only thing we know is that it was a band of witches that are unknown to all of the covens."

"You mean like from the story?" She asked our eyes meeting and I nodded, "I think it's time to show him Lana." Her gaze shifting to the vampire.

"I think so too" She grinned back.

"What have you two been up to?" I narrowed my eyes as they grinned at each other. I stood up as Katia did, Ed and Alec following our lead.

Lana pushed open the door she had been leaning against when I had topped the stairs, "Welcome to A-VEWS."

CHAPTER 8

I WALKED INTO THE large room that seemed to take up the entire top story of the building. All four walls were covered in screens, stacked three high starting from halfway up the wall. There were news stations from across the country playing on some of them. Several others had scenes from the Casino below. Under the monitors that showed the news were work stations manned by several people. The lower monitors by the work stations also seemed to have articles that the people were scrolling through. In the center of the room was a large four-sided tower that ran from floor to ceiling. On two sides were whiteboards that had scrawled notes in different hand writings, and on the other two sides were cork boards with what looked like article printouts pinned to them. I stepped forward to read one of the print outs when I recognized the name of the area we had found the Garnet Alter at the month before. It was about a small fire that no body could explain, about how it had taken the authorities nearly a full day plus to put it out. I hadn't even thought about the fire when we were leaving that day. My only thought had been to get Gideon somewhere to help his i   n   -juries.

"What is this place?" I asked turning to look at the two girls who stood on either side of the door we had come In through, both of them grinning like proud parents on Christmas morning.

"Alliance of Vampires, Elves, Witches, and Shifters. A-VEWS for Short" Katia said stepping forward, "It's what we always talked about growing up Zander. Is a group where all the species work together to help each other."

"We are still small, only seven of us." Lana continued, "Other than me and Katia we have two shifters, two Elves, and another Vampire."

"No one in the coven knows I'm part of this, Marilyn has actually forbidden anyone from the coven to even contact A-VEWS." Katia said shaking her head, "the same way she always forbids anyone from reaching out to any of the other covens."

"Marilyn is a fool." I spit out rolling my eyes.

"Wait, your High Priestess has forbidden your coven from contacting other covens?" Randall said stepping back toward the group from where he had wondered to look at the extensive set up.

"When we were growing up we were always told anyone outside the coven was a danger. That only coven members could be trusted and that they would protect us." I said looking over at him, "they said that about sixty years ago another coven attacked ours. The only reason the coven was barely affected and not completely wiped out was that the High Priestess at the time had a Premonition warning of the attack months in advance. The Elders all worked on a cloaking spell to hide us from the attacking coven and that was when the coven began making defensive potions and we have been ever since."

"How are you getting away with being here if Marilyn forbid it? I know dad would never let you go against the coven's orders." I asked looking at my sister.

"I work as a dealer in the Casino below," she shrugs, "If we have things going on with A-VEWS I just tell dad that I'm picking up extra shifts. A-VEWS owns the Casino under a cover name, so we just doctor my paychecks when needed."

"What all do you do with A-VEWS?" Alec asked as he paced the room his eyes scanning everything, and I knew that if I asked him later he would be able to give me a detailed description of everything.

"Whatever the paranormal community needs," Lana answered, "mostly we help shifters and vampires who are rogues, who don't have a pack or house to turn to. Most people don't know about us right now," she shrugged, "so we don't have the backing of any of the officials from any of the groups and none of them turn to us."

"Eventually what we hope to do," Katia said stepping next to Lana, "is to work with the houses, packs, covens and the elves to set up at least one office in each region with a central headquarters somewhere in the middle of the country. I was going to ask you to talk to the Guardians to see if they could help us with the Covens. Now with the Guardians dead I'm not sure how we can approach all the covens on even footing." She sent a nervous glance at Lana.

"What about the shifters and the elves?" Ed asked joining the conversation.

"The shifters have a gathering of the leaders once a quarter," A young woman said rolling her chair over to joining us. Her brown and gold hair was cut short to her head and spiked up in every direction. She had amber-colored eyes behind thick glasses and there was a small diamond stud in her sloped nose. "I'm going to head to the next meeting to talk with them. I'm Eliza by the way," she grinned and reached up to shake each of our hands.

"Nice to meet you Eliza, I'm Zander. This is Ed, Randall, and Alec." I introduced each as she shook their hands.

"I am working to get a hold of the House of Ophiuchus to get the vampires on board," Lana said.

"The elves are a little harder with the turmoil that's happening with them." Katia cut in, "but we will be working to try to get them to join as well. Once we have everyone on board we can make things so much easier on the entire paranormal community."

"So, if you get everyone on board then what?"

"Well then," Lana shrugged, "anything really. We can help mediate disagreements between factions, we can help lost paranormals, anything really."

"You guys will be what just a neutral place for everyone?" Ed asked.

"Exactly, but in cases like this we could reach out to the houses and packs and see if they had noticed anything. With how things are right now we have no way to reach out to them." Eliza said with a shrug, "No way to see if they know anything."

I looked at the others, "we could talk to the others back," I hesitated remembering at the last minute not to say where we had holed up, "at base and see what they think."

"What all would we need to start somethin' like this?" Randall asked.

"Someplace to act as a front, like we use the casino here. When people start to congregate regularly somewhere new it tends to draw attention. With the paranormal community in hiding, we don't want to draw attention to ourselves. If we start to do that then no one will trust us." Lana said.

"What about a bar?" Ed asked from where he leaned against one of the low counters.

"A bar would work, would also explain why there are people there so late at night," Eliza said with a nod.

"You also need to recruit at least one of each type of paranormals, vampires, shifters, and elves." Katia said, "You'll have witches."

"I'm not sure we can trust the elves in the area we are," Randall said looking at all of us.

"I agree they can't be trusted." Alec nodded.

"You will need to find some that you can trust. In order for this to work, you would need equal representation." Katia said shaking her head.

"We will call the others and discuss it with them in the morning." Ed said stopping the bickering before it could get started, "We should get back to your place soon though."

"Before you leave, what types of things can we look for to help locate these artifacts?" Eliza asked as she sat at the closest workstation.

"Look for signs people knew something was going to happen before it did. Underdogs that came out on top, someone coming into money they shouldn't have," I said, "It could honestly be anything."

"I can look over any articles you come up across and see if we can find a pattern" Katia nodded at the shifter.

"Katia, we still need to go talk to the Coven. What we learned here has helped, but I think the key is with Marilyn and her stories." I said.

"I'll try to get something set up for tomorrow." I hugged Katia and Lana and shook Eliza's hand before I led the troops back down the stairs.

When we got back to my apartment, we sat around my coffee table with Randall's phone laying on it, the speaker on and ringing.

"Randy?" Gwen's voice floated from the phone. We all looked at Randall and I grinned when I saw his cheeks had reddened. I had known there was something between them.

"Gwen, you're on speaker. We need to talk to everyone at the house, can you get them?"

"Give me just a minute and I will see who all I can gather, I believe a few of the girls went out shopping though." The phone was silent for several minutes, "Ok, you have me, Jamal, Esme, and Gideon here." Gwen came back.

"What's going on? Have you found the mirror?" Gideon's voice was hopeful.

"No, this isn't about the artifacts," I answered quickly, "not directly at least."

"Then why are we discussing it?" he snapped.

"It's not directly linked to the artifacts, but this could help us find the artifacts and keep the peace after." I explained calmly, "we talked to an old friend of mine here in Vegas. She is a vampire, who has started an alliance with a few local shifters, elves, and my sister. They want to set up similar alliances throughout the country. We were thinking that it may be convenient to have one near the new Sacred Space."

"And how is this useful in finding the artifacts?" Jamal asked.

"The more people we have connections with, the more alliances we have, the more people who can look for the artifacts and the faster we can retrieve them all," I said.

"And you are wanting to set up a division here in New Orleans?" Gwen asked.

"We think it would be a good move on a lot of fronts." Randall cut in, "not only would we have allies looking for the artifacts, but we can also keep an eye on the other species through the alliance."

"We don't need you guys to do anything other than talking it over and think about it," I said, not wanting to draw out the conversation over the phone when we didn't have someone from A-VEWS here with us to help explain how helpful it would be to start one up. "once we get back to New Orleans we can figure out what we will do next."

"Have you had any leads on the mirror?" Gideon asked, frustration clear in his voice.

"We talked to the alliance here. They are going to reach out and scan the net to see what they can find," I answered and swallowed the lump forming in my throat, "tomorrow we are going to go talk to my old coven."

"Keep us informed," Gwen said, "blessed be." she whispered before ending the call.

CHAPTER 9

W E PULLED UP OUTSIDE the old adobe colored house with red shutters lining the windows. The front had a large circular two-story porch with wrought iron railings between the tall pillars and a sweeping staircase to the right that lead from the drive way up to the porch. Looking at the old house I could feel my pulse speeding up and had to close my eyes and take calming breaths. I had to push away the memories that being back here brought on.

"You ok?" Alec asked softly as the other two got out of the back seat of the van, their familiars following them.

"A lot of bad memories here," I muttered.

"Nothing else will happen here today." He said, setting his hand on my shoulder. I smiled at him before we both got out of the car.

"Everything ok?" Ed asked.

"Yup," I forced a grin at them and led the group up the arching stairs. As I reached the top, I couldn't help but flashback to when Katia and I used to play on the rough stone of the porch floor. Laying out tarot spreads with old decks of playing cards, pretending to read each other's future. Taking a deep breath I continued to the front door and pressed the button for the doorbell. I waited until the rust red door was opened by a Marilyn much older than I remembered. Her once dark brown hair was now a pearly silver, and she had deep wrinkles on her forehead between her dark grey eyes. The hand that she used to open the door was wrinkled with large veins on top.

"Welcome back home child," Her voice was the same as when I was growing up but I had a hard time reconciling it to the old woman standing in front of me with the once elegant matriarch I had known as a child. It had been over 20 years since I had last laid eyes on my High Priestess.

"Thank you for the welcome Marilyn, but this is no longer my home." I smiled gently at her to soften the words as we walked in. I no longer held ill will towards her or the rest of the coven for not stepping in with my father, and I wanted her to know that. Once we were all inside the small front foyer, she led us to the sitting room off to the right. It hadn't changed one bit since I had last been here. Inside the room was the old cherry wood coffee table polished to a gleam. In the center of the table was a large vase filled with a mix of the round pink, white, and purple althea flowers and a scattering of the bright blue star-shaped borage flowers. Around the flowers hanging over the vase were masses of long lemongrass leaves. Opposite the entrance on the other side of the table was an old stone fireplace, the hearth scared with marks of black from past fires. On one side of the table was an old black velvet couch with ornate cherry wood arms, legs, and back carvings. Across from this were two matching high-back chairs.

My pulse sped and my breath caught in my throat when I looked at the chairs. Sitting in the one closest to the fireplace, facing the entryway was my father, Virgil. Katia was standing at his back, hands resting on the back of the chair, one over the other. Her eyes were weary, and I knew that she had tried to keep my father from being here today. Like Merlyn, he had aged since I had last seen him. His dark hair was now streaked in grey, the hair at his temples now more grey than black. His dark black-brown eyes were still as cold as I remember them being the morning he had kicked me out of the house, and still filled with the loathing I had seen in them most of my childhood.

"Father," I nodded at him. I waited till Marilyn had taken a seat in the chair next to his before moving to sit in the center of the couch. Ed and Randall sat on either side of me, Alec taking up station behind us.

"How can we help you?" Marilyn asked.

"Do you remember the story you used to tell all the coven children about the Guardians and ancient artifacts that they protected?"

"Oh for the love of the god and goddess," my father growled, "you abandoned your mission over some stupid children's story?"

"Shut up for once in your life," I replied not taking my eyes from Marilyn, "do you remember the story?"

"How dare you" he roared surging to his feet.

"Virgil sit down," Marilyn said a flick of her hand in his direction silencing him, "Of course, twelve guardians for twelve artifacts dating back to the witch trials."

"Was there anything missing from that story? We know that there are eleven covens besides ours, but could there be another?"

"Why do you think that?" She asked moving to sit on the edge of her seat.

"Representatives from all twelve covens showed up in the clearing. But there was a thirteenth group who was there before us. They killed the guardians and took the artifacts."

"Are you saying the artifacts and the guardians are all real?" My father demanded.

"Why do you think your powers stopped working?" I finally looked at him, "unfortunately the goddess doesn't take away powers just because you are a shitty person and a sorry excuse of a parent."

"That is enough," Marilyn's voice cut between us like a whip, "Zander, what are you asking?"

"I need to know if there was another coven back in Salem. If not, could there have been other witches in neighboring towns back then? If they weren't in Salem, then we need to know where they came from."

"You are sure that they are not one of the twelve?" She asked standing to pace the small room.

"Yes, the others are all as in the dark as we are. One of the twelve gave up their life for one of the artifacts and another was gravely injured," I watched her pace as I relayed the information.

"As far as I know there were only twelve families, twelve artifacts. I can read through the old grimoires and journals in the coven library. See if I can find any reference to a thirteenth family, coven, power, or artifact."

"We appreciate it. We are all reaching out to our covens to see if they can find any reference to these witches," Alec said from behind me. "Once we know who and what we are fighting it will make it easier." We stood from where we had sat and all headed toward the door. I held the door open for the others and kissed Marilyn on the cheek as was customary in the coven. I may not have been apart of the Seers Circle in two decades but old habits died hard.

The door opened behind us moments after it closed. I turned to find my father exiting, Katia scurrying after him, eye filled with fear.

"You are an ungrateful, disgrace of a son." He spat stalking toward me.

"And you are a piece of shit human being," I narrowed my eyes at him. I was no longer the young boy who cowered in the face of this man's rage. I stepped back as he swung his fist at my jaw as he had so many times in the past. Before I could react, Alec had him pushed against one of the porch columns, his arm pressed against his throat, my father's toes barely touching the ground.

"You need to learn to keep your hands and opinions to yourself," Alec growled into my father's face.

"Go figure, my fairy of a son brought another fag home with him." my father wheezed out.

"Alec, he isn't worth it," I set a hand on his barely straining arm. He stepped back letting the older man collapse to the ground. We both turned our backs on him to follow the others to the van. We hadn't taken more than two steps when Alec ducked my father's fist before turning back around and hitting him square in the jaw. He fell flat on his back on the porch moaning, hand coming up to cup his jaw. We left him there like that and all piled back into the van to head back to my apartment.

Chapter 10

THE NEXT NIGHT I made the others the steaks I had stock piled in my freezer while we waited till full dark to head back to the Four Queens casino. This time we decided to bring the familiars with us so knew a cab was out of the question. We ended up piling into the van to make our way through downtown. It took nearly twenty minutes for us to get to the casino where we were let into the small employee parking lot in the back by an older gentleman in a small guard shack. We all walked to the side of the building and gave the door a few hard raps to the metal door. Within seconds Eliza, the shifter from two nights ago, opened the door to allow us into the building. We all filed up the stairs where she unlocked the door.

"Come on in, Lana said she's expecting you." She grinned over her shoulder and led us to the center of the room where Lana was waiting for us. I hugged Lana when I got to her before looking around the room, something inside twisting when I didn't see my sister there also.

"Katia isn't coming in, she said to tell you everything is ok though," Lana said noticing my searching gaze. I nodded my head in thanks feeling a weight lift from my shoulders.

"So, any luck?" I asked dropping into the metal chair at head of the folding table that had been brought in since our last visit. It was sitting off to the side of the middle column between it and the workstations along the wall.

"Sadly, we've had no luck on many fronts," Lana said sitting opposite end of the table as me, the others filling in on either side of the table between us.

"What do you mean?" Alec asked from next to me on my right.

"Well, to start we haven't picked up anything online that seems to point to people having premonitions." She said.

"We haven't found anything yet," Eliza called from where she had taken up residence back at her workstation.

"Yes, we haven't found anything yet." Lana rolled her eyes, "But I also haven't been able to get ahold of the House of Ophiuchus either."

"Have you reached out to any of the other houses to see if they have heard from them?" I asked.

"Wait," Ed asked holding up a hand to interrupt, "who is the House of Ophiuchus?" He asked looking between us. I tilted my head towards Lana giving her the floor.

"The vampires here in the US are divided amongst house based on their abilities. Each house has a nominated vampire that is transferred to the House of Ophiuchus. They are the governing body for vampires. The House is judge, jury, and executioner for vampires. If you break the rules and they find you guilty, they will kill you before you even know that you committed the crime."

"That seems a little harsh," Randall said lifting a brow.

"We are vampires, we don't have the luxury of being gentle or forgiving. One vampire in blood lust can kill over 100 people in one night. We can't afford to have the fact that we exist made known to the world. You thought the witch trials in Salem were gruesome? You should see what they did to suspected vampires in Europe in the 1500s. Even worse was when a 'Doctor' would get his hands on a real vampire." She looked away and I could see her shudder. It was then that I realized I didn't know how old Lana was and had never thought to ask, "They tried to learn what made us tick. What kept us alive when we should have been dead. How to kill us so we were dead. What didn't kill some of us but killed others. When the new world was discovered we came here eagerly and in droves that were nearly double that of the human settlers. We came here in hopes that we would never suffer that type of fear and agony again. That is why our justice system is so harsh. None of us want to think about what would happen in modern times if the hunts started again, if the knowledge those doctors," she snarled the word, "was brought to light again. Now when there are so many new things they can do to us. The new ways that today's scientists could experiment," she closed her eyes, lips pressing together as she fought through her own fear. I wanted to reach out and comfort her, but didn't dare show that weakness to the strangers in this room, "I don't even want to imagine those horrors. We already had a scare here in the United States in the 1800s.

Back then they would inject us with holy water that burned through our veins like acid. That was bad enough to witness. I know of some who were staked hands and feet before vivisected while awake and screaming. They would heal during the day while they slept and the scientists would start again when they woke up." She looked back to us, her eyes filled with raw pain and fear, "Even now I know that certain sectors of the humans Government have found out about us and begun the experimenting again. Did you know that certain UV bulbs work on us same as the sun does? We can't go near tanning beds, even some SADS lamps will burn us." The last words were whispered. She closed her eyes again and took a deep breath, "So yes, the House is harsh, but they are also protective of us. They care about their houses and to have a call go unanswered for longer than a night is unheard of."

"Ok, so where is the House of Ophiuchus located?" Ed asked.

"On the East coast," she stood from the table and paced. I watched as she started to chew on the side of her left thumb, her right arm crossed over her body, left elbow resting on the palm of her right hand, it was as if she were fighting not to hug herself. After a few minutes she looked back at us, "I don't know how much I can tell you. We don't like to let it be known where our houses are, it's another way to keep everyone safe, fanged and none fanged alike. What I can tell you is that there are twelve houses, thirteen if you include the House of Ophiuchus."

"We can't help you if we don't know anything," Alec said gently.

"I have to talk to a few others. I'm already in the trouble with my house because I went against my leaders' orders to start the alliance. If I tell you anything and they find out, they may just stake me out in the yard for the sun to take care of." While her words came out as casual I could hear the tension in my old friends voice.

"We wouldn't let them do that Lana, I wouldn't let them do that," I said standing and moving to my old friend.

"You wouldn't have a choice. One day I would be here and the next I wouldn't. It's not like they would give us a warning." She took another deep breath before looking past me at the others, "for now though we need more information about the mirror. Things we need to look for."

"Can I put out a suggestion?" Eliza asked turning from her workstation.

"Of course," Randall answered as we all moved to stand around her chair.

She pushed her glasses up higher on her nose as she stood, "what if we are going about this all wrong. We have been looking for a grouping of these instances in small clusters, which we haven't found, but what if they aren't sticking to one town or even county?"

"What are you suggesting?"

"You guys told me to look for things like a bet on an underdog that came out on top, people coming into money that they probably shouldn't have. Katia suggested looking for instances where someone knew to buy or sell stocks even when it didn't make sense. So we can assign each of those a different color pin and also add in another color for other 'lucky' streaks," she air quoted lucky, "Then we can take all the articles and intelligence we have gathered and put them up on a map. Maybe then we can find a larger pattern that's harder to trace when we aren't looking at specific town and city names."

"That's a really good idea," Alec said frowning just a little at the small shifter, as if he was trying to see inside her head.

"I agree," Randall said running a hand over his hair, "how soon can we do this?"

"We can get started on it now. But honestly with all the instances, we found that fit your guy's very broad examples? It's going to take at least the rest of tonight and all day tomorrow if we have our day shift work on this also."

"Well then, let's get to work." Lana said walking over to an empty workstation, "we will call you when we have all the information pinned up and we can look it over together."

I walked over and pressed a kiss to the top of her head, "let us know when you need us back here. And please let me know if we can help you at all."

We all headed back down the stairs, "so back to the apartment for another night?" Randall asked.

I checked my watch and grinned back at them, "only to drop off the familiars. Tonight I show you the strip."

Chapter 11

WHEN WE GOT BACK to the apartment instead of hitting the strip with Alec and me, Ed and Randall decided to stay. They wanted to make calls to their covens to see if they could tell them anything about a thirteenth coven and then to New Orleans to update everyone. I stayed down to call an uber to take us to our first destination while Alec used my keys to let the others into the apartment and dropping off Dazzle and Crotone.

"So, anything you have been dying to see here in Vegas?" I grinned over at him when I hear the door close to the building.

"You're the native, shouldn't you know all the hot spots?" He grinned back at me and I had to count to ten.

"Alright big boy, strap in because you are in for one hell of a night." I grinned back as the black shiny Uber pulled up to the curb. The drive back was short and the silent air slowly charged with anticipation. When we got back to the strip, I grabbed his hand and dragged him out of the back seat. I weaved my way through the crowd until we came to the queue for the zip line.

"What are we waiting in this line for?"

"You will have just have to wait and see." I grinned over at him. It took us about an hour in line during which time we watched the people bustling around us. Slowly we shifted closer so by the time the check in booth came into view I was leaning against his chest, his chin resting on my shoulder.

"The zipline?" Alec asked, his voice in my ear was filled with amusement.

"It's the best way to see Fremont Street." I grinned at him as the assistants strapped us into our harnesses. I felt my heart race as we stepped up to the edge of the platform and they latched us onto the lines. As they lowered the door I looked down at the arched roof over the street that I had spent so many nights on and everything went still. Alec and I moved forward together, stepping off the platform. Then we were soaring through the night. We glided into the tunnel of lights, people moving below us. I looked over and beamed at Alec who smiled back. For those short 30 seconds that we were in the air I let myself forget everything that was falling apart around us. We came to a stop over the other platform and the world seemed to rush back into life around us, pulling us from the momentary bubble of solitude.

Alec was grinning as we headed back down to the street level, "What's next?"

"How do you feel about the circus?"

He lifted an eyebrow, "I love it."
***

We made our way down the strip, and I loved watching Alec's face as he took everything in. As we crossed the highway I pulled him away from the front of the hotel and instead down one of the almost alley like areas that were used for deliveries.

"Zander, what are we doing?"

"We are going to see the show," I smirked at him as I found the correct door and rapped my knuckles on the cold metal.

"Shouldn't we be in the front then?"

Before I could answer him the door opened and a small man in all black peaked out, "Long time Z." he grinned as he held the door open for us. I grabbed Alec's hand and dragged him into the building when he hesitated.

"Thanks for this Zeke, it means a lot." I smiled at the man as we bumped fists, "normal seats?"

"You know it." I pulled Alec by his hand as I wove my way through the back end of the stage area and up a ladder.

"Zander what are we doing here?" he hissed quietly.

"We are going to our seats to water the show." I said as we made it to where two small X's had been marked in tape. I sat on the small ledge, letting my legs dangle as I leaned on the small railing. We were slightly off to the side of the stage and up on one of the cat walks that was only used for set up, the best seats in the house in my opinion.

"Are you sure we are supposed to be here?"

"Zeke is the head stage manager, he pulled some strings for me now sit down, people are going to start coming in." Without another word he sat next to me and we watched as people began to fill the theatre below.

***

I spent most of the show watching Alec's face as he watched the show below us, and every time I saw the awe on his face I felt myself falling for him a little more. At the end of the finale, I laughed when he pressed his pinkies to his lips and let out a piercing whistle. We waited until the crowd below started to file out before we made our way from our seats.

"That was, amazing." Alec laughed when we exited the back of the the-ater and into the night air. "What's next?"

"Come on." I grabbed his hand and dragged him down the street and to the front of the Casino until we stood in front of the Bellagio fountains.

It only took him a few minutes be-fore he turned to look at me, "Is the water dancing?" Alec asked in aston-ishment.

"It is." I smiled when he slipped his arm over my shoulder and I curled into his side to watch the show.

***

We both stumbled from the car laughing, holding each other up with an arm around each other's waist. We walked to the doors still giggling like schoolboys, leaning heavily on one another. As I fumbled with my keys, I felt a hand on my shoulder and Alec's voice rumbled in my ear, "Zan-der?" I turned back around to look at him and found myself flattened against the door his mouth fused to mine. I groaned pushing my hands to his chest before fisting his shirt and yanking him harder against me. I wanted to melt into him when I felt one of his hands reach up to fist in my hair and growled when I remembered that his was too short to return the favor. He pulled back from the kiss pulling my bottom lip with his teeth, "Thanks for the night out." He whispered dark eyes on my own.

I pressed myself against him a little harder, "the pleasure was mine," my voice was raspy as I responded. He reached around me and turned the key I had gotten in the door, opening it and holding it open for us. We walked up the stairs, him reaching forward to hold my hand, and continued down the hallway side by side. When we went into the apartment the lights were off and I could see the others passed out on the couches, "you want the floor in here or to join me in my nice comfy king-sized bed?" I whispered to him.

"Lead the way seer" he smiled.

Chapter 12

I WOKE UP TO my phone buzzing along the top of my dresser, Alec's arm heavy over my waist holding me against the hard warmth of his body. I grabbed blindly for my phone and answered it before bringing it to my ear, "Hello?" I grumbled, snuggling back into Alec even as his arm tightened around me.

"Why are you still sleeping?" Katia's voice rang in my ear, "It's nearly 10."

"Yeah, and we have only been in bed for like four hours." I snapped back. I hated mornings with a passion, always had while she had always been a morning person.

"We huh?" I could hear the smirk in her voice, "Please tell me it was that Latino hunk."

"Good-Bye Kat" I hung up the phone and tossed it to the side of the bed.

"Someone's grumpy in the mornings." Alec's sleep deepened voice in my ear sent shivers down my spine.

"Damn straight I am" I growled rolling over in his arms and pressing my mouth to his. Just as I slipped my arms around him there was a banging on the door.

"Will you two get out here? We aren't going to listen to you go at it like a couple of teenagers on Prom Night." Randall's voice boomed through the door.

I flopped onto my back with a groan, "We could pretend to be asleep still." I whispered in response to Alec's soft chuckle.

"The things I would do to you, no one would believe you were asleep" His laugh as he slid from the bed sent shiver down my spine. I watched appreciatively as he pulled his jeans on, tightening the belt around his slim waist. "Stop staring, and get up and dressed." He grinned over his shoulder.

"Party pooper," I muttered and sat up stretching, twisting just a little to pop my back.

"You'll live." He snorted softly. I made my way over to my dresser to dig out clothes. I pulled a faded grey

T-shirt from the second drawer, sliding it on before heading toward the closet. "Hey, Zander," Alec called just before I opened the door.

"Hmm?" I turned to face him only to find myself shoved flat against the door of my closet. His hips grinding hard against mine pinning them in place. One hand was fisted in my hair the other cupping the side of my throat, his thumb guiding my chin up. When I opened my mouth to say, I wasn't sure what, only to have his mouth fasten to mine. By the time he pulled his lips from mine, I could only make small noises that were nowhere near intelligent words. I stared up into his dark brown eyes and the rest of the world faded away.

"Deep breaths Love," he whispered softly, only causing my breath to catch again, "that was only a kiss and I want to do so much more to you." His promise of more had me closing my eyes as I tried to follow his order to breathe. The man was going to kill me. The hand at my throat slid around to the back of my neck and he pulled my head down to rest on his shoulder. He pressed a kiss to my temple before he laid his cheek against mine. I slid my arms around him pulling him against me.

When both of our breathing evened out I lifted my head and brushed my lips against his again, "We should finish getting ready before they start pounding on the door again." I whispered against his lips.

"Soon we are going to find time to be alone in private," he growled before nipping hard at my bottom lip.

We left the bedroom a few minutes later hand in hand to find Randall leaning against the counter and Ed looking out the window, both with steaming mugs of what I could only assume was coffee.

"Have we heard anything yet?" Ed said turning to look at us.

"My sister called a little bit ago. I'll give her a callback and see if they have anything, But Lana won't be available until after dusk." I reminded heading into the kitchen. I grabbed a glass from the cabinet and held it up to Alec questioningly. When he shook his head no, I closed the cabinet, grabbed the pitcher of water from the fridge and poured myself a glass. Once the pitcher was put back in the fridge, I hopped up on one of the counters and hit my sister's name in my phone. I gulped down the icy water as I listened to the phone ringing in my ear.

"Done getting your jollies little brother?" Her voice was cocky when she answered.

"Bite me Kat," I rolled my eyes as I set the glass on the counter next to me, "Why did you wake me up this morning?"

"We think we may have something. Lana wanted you guys here as soon as the sun's down so that we can look over everything."

"Do you think you found the right place?"

I heard her sigh in frustration and could picture her fisting her hair and giving it a light tug like she did when frustrated, "Maybe? It's hard to say. We definitely found an interesting pattern of events that should be looked into. Unfortunately, nothing where we can say for sure 'look here for mirror'. It could be a group of coincidences or it could be where the mirror is located." It was strange for my sister to be so indecisive.

"Ok, we will be there at dusk," I assured her. I hesitated a moment before asking, "Have you heard anything from Marilyn?"

"Nothing, but I'll let you know as soon as I do if she calls."

"Alright, I'll see you in a few hours."

"So what's the word?" Randall asked. I looked up and they were all watching me expectantly.

"They think they may have found a pattern. Kat wants us to wait until Lana is available so we can all look over things." I said with a shrug, "so we have roughly eight hours to kill." Just as I finished talking, Randall's phone started to ring.

"Gwen, what's wrong?" his voice was gruff, and immediately I was on alert along with the others. I slid from the counter and moved closer. "One moment and I will put the phone on speaker." We all headed into the living room and he set the phone on the coffee table turning it to speaker, "Ok go ahead."

"Hey boys," Gwen's voice rang out through the speaker.

"Hey, Gwen, what's up?" I asked trying not to let the fact that Alec pulled me onto his lap be reflected in my voice.

"We have been talking about setting up an A-VEWS office down here." Jamal's thick southern voice came over the speaker.

"And?" I slid to the end of Alec's lap.

"Well, we think it would be a good idea. We also all agreed that we can't take the time out from looking for the Artifacts to set this up and also run the day-to-day operations," Misty answered.

"What if we can get someone from the Las Vegas office to come down and work the New Orleans office until we get the artifacts set up and reinstate Guardians?" Ed asked and I nodded at him.

"Do you have someone who you trust?" Gideon asked.

"There are several who I trust," I answered thinking of Lana and my sister.

"Would one of them be willing to come down here?" Gwen asked.

"We can ask them tonight. They think they may have found something to help us locate the mirror," I said.

"Let us know what you find out," Gideon said before the call ended. We all looked at each other in the resulting silence.

"I don't know about you guys but I'm going back to get a few more hours of sleep." I said removing myself from Alec's lap, "Feel free to raid the fridge or order take out.

Eight hours later we once again pulled into the employee lot and made our way up the stairs to what I was starting to think of as the war room. I knocked on the door once before opening it and leading the way in. A large rolling cork board had been wheeled into the room and had multi colored pins scattered across it. Walking closer I could see that there were large clusters along the upper east coast, specifically around a small bay area.

"I see that you are seeing what we did," Lana said turning from her workstation.

"East Coast," I said with a nod.

Katia joined me at the board, "specifically around this tiny bay here in Rhode Island." She traced her finger over the tops of the pins.

"Are we thinking that's where the mirror is?" Ed asked.

"As of right now it's our best guess." Lana nodded.

"Can we digitize this?" Alec asked from just behind me."

"Already done," Eliza said from her station, "just need to know the email to send it to."

"Can I use a computer?" I asked nodding to the stations around the room.

"Go for it," Lana said. I sat at a computer and pulled up google. After a few tries, I had an account created.

"Send it to ArtifactSearchers12@g mail.com," I said turning to Eliza.

"You got it boss man," she grinned and pushed her glasses farther up her nose as she turned to her computer.

"Now that that's settled we have a few other things to talk to you guys about," I said turning to face the group again.

"What's up?" Lana asked leaning her hip onto one of the desks.

"We got a call from the others back at the house this morning. They like the idea of having an A-VEWs office near where we are, but they don't want to pull away from the search for the artifacts to run it. We would take it over once we have the Artifacts and get all the powers back online for everyone. So, what they want to know," I looked at Katia hopefully. Secretly I hoped that she would agree to come back with us because Goddess, I had missed my sister, "Is if one of you could come down to help us to get things off the ground and moving there."

"I can't leave here, I'm the only witch we have until we can get Marilyn on board." She said, and I could hear the regret in her voice.

"I'm the head of the location here, I can't leave for more than a day or two," Lana said. I deflated back into the chair disappointed. If not Katie, I had hoped for Lana to come back with us.

"What about Eliza?" Katia asked Lana.

"She would be a great option, since she knows all the ins and outs and is really good with supernaturals." Lana nodded, "Hey Eliza, can you join us over here?" She called to the shifter.

With a push of her feet, her chair glided over to the small group, "What's up boss?"

"How would you like to go on a little business trip?" Lana grinned.

Chapter 13

I SAT IN THE passenger seat with Alec driving, Randall and Ed had taken up residence in the middle seat. Eliza was in the far back with the Familiars, minus Dazzle, who had all flocked to her. Dazzle had opted to sprawl on the dash so he could sun himself. We had picked up an overhead luggage rack since we had extra bags and needed an extra seat.

"So where are we going?" Eliza asked.

"New Orleans," Randall replied.

"Wait, you guys are hiding the witch headquarters in New Orleans?" I turned in my seat and watched her amber eyes dart between all of us a slow grin spreading across her face, "That's genius! Like hiding in plain sight." She was practically vibrating in her seat. In the short time that I had known her I had come to realize she was a nerd, in the most basic sense of the word.

I laughed, "That's what we thought too. It helps that there are a few lay lines there for us to pull on."

"Witches use lay lines?" her brows crinkled.

"Not normally, but right now we can use all the help we can get until we are at full power," Ed said with a shrug.

"This is fascinating. You witches are probably the most secretive group in the supernatural world." Her face scrunched up as she thought about it, "well not including the vampires, or the elves." She gave a small laugh, "I guess us shifters are the only ones who don't guard every little thing like a secret."

"That happens when everyone still remembers the last time we were hunted," Alec said softly. We all went silent, the images seen in Salem still fresh.

"What's it like not having your powers?" She asked. I could see the itch for her to pull out a notebook to take notes as if in a lecture.

"We still have some powers, but not our major ones." I said with a shrug, "Think of it this way. Imagine that you can still shift into your animal form, but you lose your other abilities. Your vision is only as good as your animal form, your sense of smell is only as good as your animal form. You no longer have extraordinary speed or strength, because you have lost whatever ability it is that your tribe has."

She sat and thought about that for a minute, "I think it would feel like losing half of myself, like I wasn't complete." She looked up at me, her eyes had a touch of fear in them at the thought of it.

I nodded, "Exactly. You can survive like that but you would always feel like something was missing. We can survive without our major powers. We are surviving, but we would never feel like whole without returning the major powers to us." The car was silent as we all thought over what I had just said. Went quiet as the thought of not being able to get our powers settled over us.

"A-VEWS will help you get them back, I will help you get them back." She said fiercely and in that moment I could see the predator in her eyes.

"Don't promise that," Alec said softly. He looked back and I saw him catch her eyes in the rearview mirror, "while we all want our powers back, we can live without them. And they are not worth any more innocent lives."

***

As the sun set, I leaned against Alec and laid my head on his shoulder with a yawn. We had switched with Randall and Ed about an hour before and I felt drained.

"You should sleep," His voice was soft as to not wake Eliza who had lade down the back seat again and was curled up with the familiars in a big puppy pile.

"I know, just can't help but thinking about what Kenna's poor family must be going through. She seemed to be pretty close to them from what I gathered during our time together."

He was silent for a few minutes, his head resting against mine. "When we get back to New Orleans, I think we should bring it up to the others, calling her family. We need at least one person from her coven to come and set up portals at headquarters. None of us are that skilled in the Astral Planes. And then they could see her, perform any last rights that they normally would."

"She isn't dead yet," I argued.

"I know that. Hopefully we will be able to wake her," He lifted the arm I was leaning on and wrapped it around my shoulders pulling me in

to rest against his chest, "but until we find the Mirror you need to rest." He ordered before laying his head on mine. Turning my face into his chest I closed my eyes and let the motion and noise of the car lull me to sleep.
  ***
I woke up to the sound of Alec's deep voice and a less familiar soft feminine voice. I shifted in the constrains of my seat to nuzzle my face into the hard chest. Slowly I opened my eyes and tilted my head, my eyes meeting Alec's warm brown laughing ones, "good morning sunshine, we didn't mean to wake you."

"Do you ever sleep?" I grumbled, pressing my face back against his chest.

"The military pretty much gets rid of that instinct," he chuckled and ran a hand through my hair. I sat up and stretched as best I could in the confines of the van.

"And what is the topic of choice and way too freaking early this morning?" the end of my sentence came out a muffled yawn.

"Eliza there was just telling us some more information about shifters," Randall said from his spot in the driver's seat. Ed was pressed against the passenger side window snoring lightly.

"Awesome, fill me in." I grinned as I settled back in against Alec's chest. I smiled contently when he rested his chin on my shoulder.

She smiled at me, "I was explaining to them that being a shifter is different than how the witches and seems like the vampires, and apparently the elves, all are. We have our packs that we can default to but for the most part we each live our own lives separately. We can go to our pack when ever and for anything but we don't expect anything in return from other pack members when they ask for help. We have a loose power structure, but mostly its so that we can have the lands we use held under a name."

"What about the shifting?" Alec asked.

"There really isn't much to it," she shrugged, "it gets a little warm, the magic fills us and then we are our animal. When we want to turn back we can pull on the magic, and poof we are human." She grimaced, "Though for som reason we never seem to be able to keep our clothes when we shift. We all just carry extras with us in case we have to shift."

"What is it like in animal form?" Ed asked.

She thought about that a minute, "nothing really changes. We have all the same sense in human form. the biggest difference for me is that when I shift I can fly." I sat and thought about what it would have be like to soar high above everything, to escape the bull shit.

"What's that like?" I asked.

"Alec mentioned that you guys went on the zipline in Vegas?"

I felt myself frown at the change of topic but nodded, "Yeah, I thought is would be something fun for him to do as a virgin."

Alec growled from next to me, "I am in no way a virgin Seer."

Eliza and I grinned at each other, "Vegas Virgin." We said in unison before laughing.

"I wasn't changing the topic," she said as she waved away her laugh. "But flying is like that, only better. When I'm in the air, I feel weightless, and not just physically, but mentally too. You feel free, and unbound to anything on the ground. The higher you fly, the more you feel invincible." I could hear the love and yearning in her voice and for a few minutes I felt envious of the nerdy shifter.

Chapter 14

THE SUN WAS JUST hitting its peak in the sky the next day when we pulled into the back lot of the house that had become the new Sacred Space. We all climbed out of the van taking a few minutes to stretch out the stiffness from travel before we gathered our belongings from the luggage racks. The Familiars darted around the enclosed area of the back yard, joyous at the ability to stretch their legs. I smiled at their antics as we made our way passed the finished and now filled flower beds and into the house.

"Did you learn anything?" Gwen asked as she met us at the back door, holding it open for us all to file in.

I nodded, "We think we know the approximate location of the mirror."

"How long until you have it?" Gideon asked from the bottom of the stairs. I looked at him and my heart broke for him all over again. He looked like hadn't slept the whole time we had been gone, nearly a full week. His dark eyes were dull, nearly lifeless, and sunken from the dark circles under his eyes. His once well-maintained scruff had grown into a short raggedy beard and his clothes hung from his body.

"Soon. We will be leaving again in just a few days to find its exact location and retrieve it." I walked to him and set my hand on his shoulder. I lowered my voice for only him to hear, "You must take better care of yourself, my friend." I said with a soft shake of his shoulder, "Kenna will not be pleased to find you in such a state when we wake her."

He looked away and then back to me, "You think we will?" he asked, eyes pleading me to assure him.

I nodded, "we will or I will die trying."

"Don't say that. As much as I want Kenna back, she will not thank anyone for giving themselves for her," Gideon said voice soft.

"Are we still talking about Saint Kenna?" Eris snarked as she passed by the group of us.

"Well except maybe her," he said darkly, glaring at the blondes back as she went into the small parlor.

"Who is this?" Gwen asked as Eliza joined us, the Familiars following her inside.

"This is the A-VEWS advocate," Ed said as he took her bag from her.

"Eliza," she smiled taking Gwen's outstretched hand, "I am very excited to meet you all. We at A-VEWS want to help you to get your powers back."

"How much have you told her?" Misty asked from the entryway to the parlor where Eris had disappeared.

"Everything." Randall said, "We need to tell them everything in order for them to be of any use to us. We all have agreed that we must retrieve the artifacts and A-VEWS has resources that we don't have."

"Let's gather everyone into the dining room and we can all get back on the same page." Gwen urged, stopping any arguments before they could start. I smiled at her and gave her a side hug, dropping a kiss to her grey hair.

"I've missed you Gwen," I grinned down at her before heading into the dinning room with Eliza.

***

It took nearly half an hour to get us all congregated around the large table in the dining room. The fact that we still had enough chairs for everyone even with our guest there was a reminder that we had already lost one of our own.

"So Eliza," Misty said her strong voice cutting through the chatter that had begun to fill the room, "Gwen told us all about A-VEWS, or what they boys told her on their phone calls. We still aren't quite sure what you can do to help us. We don't know why we should trust you or why we should be willing to help you."

I held up a hand and stood. "Give me a moment," I pulled my laptop from the bag and turned it on pulling up the map with the multi-colored dots. I turned it to face the majority of the group, the rest having to move to see what I was showing them, "This is why we need A-VEWS. They were able to put this together in just twenty-four hours and continues to add to it even now. This is how we were able to determine that the Mirror is somewhere in this bay here in Rhode Island. They have access and connections throughout the whole country. Not to mention that the more groups we can get to agree to join A-VEWS the more those resources will grow. Without them, we still wouldn't know where the mirror is."

"Not to mention that had A-VEWS already been active, maybe we could have learned about the Elves' involvement in taking the gems from the Altar. We wouldn't have been blindsided when that elf showed up here." Randall gruffed.

"The Supernatural community has always been divided," Eliza said. Her voice was soft but strong like that of the hawk she turned into, "But in many ways that has been detrimental to us. We have all been taught not to trust the other, and sometimes that extends to those within our own species."

I nodded, "my coven won't allow their members to even reach out to other witches, let alone the rest of the supernatural community."

"This distrust, in the end, does nothing but harm us all. I talked to Kat, and then to Randall, Ed, Alec, and Zander on the way here. None of them even knew about these artifacts until the day they were crippled by their disappearance. Had the witches known how precarious their powers were they could have better protected them. We have stayed hidden for so long to protect ourselves against the humans that we won't allow ourselves to make allies with those who are fighting the same battle. We have cut ourselves off from resources that could help us."

"You say stay hidden from the humans as if you don't think we should. Does A-VEWS want to bring the supernatural into the open?" Eris asked voice suspicious.

Eliza held up her hands, "Not at all. A-VEWS only agenda is to unite the paranormal community. To provide help when there are disagreements or like in this case help when one group is in need. We only want to help everyone grow and be stronger."

"And what happens when there is an issue between groups? Say Elves and Witches? How do we know that A-VEWS will remain neutral?" Gwen asked.

"That is why every A-VEWS location needs associates from every species. That way if there is an interspecies conflict, the species not involved can take the lead. We are honestly just trying to help. We don't want to rule anyone, to make decisions for anyone. We just want to help, to give the supernatural community a place to go when things get hard." I leaned against the wall arms crossed as Eliza defended her cause. I watched as the others all considered everything she was saying. I hoped they would come to the correct decision.

"What would we need to do to make this work?" Jamal asked.

"A cover to start," Eliza said and pulled out a folder, "In Vegas we use a casino. Someone mentioned that a bar would be a good cover here. Next, we need to find local members of each group. You guys will be the witches, I can stand in for shifters until we reach out to the local group. We still need to talk to the local Vampire house and the local Elves."

"We don't trust the Elves." Gideon cut in.

Eliza shook her head, "This won't work if you can't come to an agreement with all the species." Eliza stood and held up her hand to stop any further arguments, "There is no other way. Listen, from what I heard it was witches that killed the previous guardians and took the artifacts. Does that make every witch bad? Should I not trust you because of something a witch that wasn't you did?" She paused to let her words sink in.

I stepped forward next to her, "I know that we have all been raised to be suspicious of others, but what if we are wrong? Witches have been hunted throughout history. Vampires have been hunted throughout history," I looked down at Eliza who confirmed my suspicions with a nod, "and Shifters have been hunted through-out history. I am sure that if we were to talk to the Elves we would learn that they too have been hunted as well. We have to stop seeing this as us against every single other group out there. Instead, we have to start seeing that we have allies, that we aren't alone. That it is the supernat-ural world against those who want to hurt us, to kill us, to eradicate us."

"Ok, then let's put this to a vote," Misty said, "We can't run this group as anything other than a democracy if we are to keep the peace."

"I agree," Jamal said sending a soft smile her way his Cajun flavored voice filling the room easily, "All those against starting an A-VEWS here in New Orleans Raise your hands." I watched as Eris's hands shot up closely followed by Gideon's. Then came Ade and Esme's hands, and I had to shake my head as Misty's hand joined the others. How could so many think this was a bad thing?

"Everyone who thinks that A-VEWS will be a good thing raises your hand," Jamal said in the same neutral voice. I nearly wept in relief as six hands raised in the air. Had anyone not vot-ed I wasn't sure what we would have done. But that didn't matter, the vote was on our side and A-VEWS would be starting in New Orleans.

CHAPTER 15

"OK, NOW THAT THAT'S settled there is one more thing we need to talk about," I said stepping back up to the table. I looked over at Gideon before looking away unable to see the completely shattered man in front of us, "We need to get the Astral Plane portals set up here."

"McKenna will do that when we get her back," Gideon said shaking her head.

"And if we need those portals in order to get her back?" Ade asked softly from her seat across from him. She reached out and set her hand softly on his, "Gideon we all want her back, but we are working blind here."

"Kenna should be the one doing it," Gideon's voice sounded lost as he leaned back in his chair, rubbing a hand over his tired face wearily.

"We can reach out to her family, have one of them come and set it up. They also have a right to see her," Gwen's voice was soft as she sat next to Gideon setting a hand on his shoulder. We all waited for him to listen to what we had said, for it to sink through the grief.

"I'll call and talk to her coven, but they are not taking her from here," Gideon said his voice brooked no argument.

"I think we will all agree with you there," Gwen said in her comforting voice.

"I will see what they say," With a nod, he stood and left the room. I looked at the others, wondering what had been going on since I had been gone.

"I take it he's still not handling this well?" I kept my voice low as I stepped over to where Ade and Misty were standing.

Misty shook her head, "he's convinced that once we have the artifacts back, we can bring her back." She looked at the door where he had exited. "I'm not sure how he will cope if we can't."

I dropped heavily into a chair at the thought. I let it roll through my head as Alec stepped behind me and his hands began to knead my shoulders, "I mean, I guess it might be possible, but we truly would need every artifact. Even then it won't be easy."

"Zander, maybe we should look at expanding that chart you started on our way to Vegas," Alec said giving my shoulders a slightly harder squeeze.

"What chart?" Esme asked from where she had perched herself on the edge of the table, not too far from where Jamal was sitting.

"On our way to Vegas I started brainstorming how to organize our searches. I made a list of the powers and the coven's best known for them. If I knew who came from what coven I added their name. Once I did that I asked the guys what their artifact was and added that too." I shrugged, "In the end I guess it does kinda look like a chart. I thought maybe if we all knew what we were looking for it would make it easier to figure out where they could be. Not to mention the more specific data we have the better AVEWS can help us."

"That was a very insightful idea Zander," Gwen said sending one of her soft smiles my way, "I believe I saw a large dry erase board when I was cleaning up in the basement. We can bring it up and put it in one of the common areas."

"Let us know when and we can bring it up for you," Ed said. Just then Gideon came back into the room.

"I talked to her coven, they will be sending her older brother in two days."

We all nodded in the heavy silence.

"I think maybe we all could use some down time." Randall said quietly. "We can set up the board tomorrow and I think a small work center for tracking items wouldn't be a bad idea." Again we nodded before making our way up the stairs.

When I went to head up to the third floor where I had stayed the last time we had been here Alec grabbed my arm, "You're staying with me Seer." His voice was just a touch deeper and again I felt things inside me tighten that shouldn't with how tired I was.

"And when was I going to be told about this change of living arrangements?" I asked lifting a brow.

He stepped forward, backing me against the wall. I swallowed and tried to slow my pulse as he lowered his face towards me. His voice was a whispered growl in my ear, "What do you think I was doing?" I closed my eyes and shivered as I felt his magic breathe over me.

"Well, why didn't you say so," my voice was breathier than I wanted.

When he pulled me into the room, his mouth devouring mine, I lost all thought of trying to protest.
 ***
 I snuggled into Alec's chest, letting myself listen to the beat of his heart, "Do you think we will get her back?" My voice was a whisper.
 "I think that if there is anyone who can do it, it's this group."
 "If we can't bring her back, I don't think Gideon will survive it."
 "We will find a way to help him through it if we can't bring her back. It wont be easy and it wont happen over night, but eventually he will come back to life. He may never be his old self, but with our help he can live."
 "I'm not sure living is worth it if you are missing a piece of yourself."
 "Soldiers do it all the time." His soft words had me sitting up to look at him through the dark,
 "Who did you lose?" I cupped his jaw in me hand as I saw old loss fill his eyes before he looked away.
 "Basic training can bring you together with fellow soldiers, deployment tightens those bonds. It's supposed to. When I joined I used the illusions power to hide what Crotone was, I had him look like a German Shepard and managed to get him in as a bomb dog. With him by my side I

had a major power boost and I walked through the battlefields with immunity to everything. I kept an energy field around me at all times, close to my person so no one got suspicious. The problem was, when my platoon was ambushed, I didn't have enough juice to protect any of them. My best friends were slaughtered around me, but not a single bullet touched me or Crotone. I never bothered to learn how to heal, and more than I care to think about bled out under my hands. When I was found, everyone told me how lucky I was," His voice filled with contempt, "I wasn't lucky. I was a coward who hid behind my powers while my brothers were killed around me. When I came back from that deployment my enlistment period was nearly over. I didn't reenlist and instead went home. If it hadn't been for my family bugging me day in and day out to join them for meals, or my mom asking for help around the house I would have let myself fade away. I was just getting back to myself when the powers stopped."

I laid back down next to him, this time pulling him into me and holding him tightly, "I am so sorry Alec." His arms tightened around me and I felt his hot tears fall onto my bare chest. I held him until his silent sobs had stopped, and continued to hold him until we both drifted off to sleep.

Chapter 16

Two days later we all loitered around the front of the house. We were waiting for Gideon and Jamal to get back from picking up Kenna's brother from the Airport. We'd had him fly into a Mississippi Airport less than two hours from us. We would be doing our best to keep the location of the house from him. Jamal would spend the drive wrapping him in illusions to help with this. When the car finally pulled to the curb and the doors opened. Gideon rushed around to help guide a young man the same height as he was from the car. My breath caught in my chest when I saw him, he looked so much like Kenna there was no mistaking their relation. When Jamal opened the door he staggered a little and I could see the exhaustion on his face.

Gwen rushed forward, with his familiar Amandi on her heels. As soon as the alligator pressed against his leg I watched Jamal stand just a little straighter. None of us spoke until we were in the house with the door closed behind us. When the door closed, there was a rush of magic as Jamal dropped the illusion. Kenna's brother blinked as if coming out of a dream. He looked around the room at all of us and I could see the grief in his eyes.

"Can I see her? Can I see my sister?" his voice, which held the same slight southern accent Kenna's had, shook.

I stepped forward sending a warning look towards Gideon who I could tell was poised to decline. "Of course, you can. I cannot express how sorry we are for your loss. We only knew Kenna for a short time but we all cared very deeply for her. If you would please follow me I'll take you up to the room where she is. My name is Zander," I reached my hand out to him and he shook it as if it were just habit.

"Aiden," was the only response he gave.

"I will open the ward," Gideon said. I nodded and the three of us along with Gwen made our way up the stairs.

We stopped in front of the door and Gideon laid his hand on the wood. There was a warm rush of magic through the air and when it dissipated, he stepped away, "I will wait out here." I nodded at him and squeezed his shoulder when he stepped aside for me to open the door. I stepped through the door and my chest tightened when I saw the small form on the bed covered in the thin white sheet.

Aiden walked across the room and dropped to his knees on the side of the bed, "This is not how we were supposed to end Kenna." His voice was barely loud enough to hear from where I stood near the door, "It was supposed to be me and you running the coven in another twenty years. How am I supposed to take care of everyone without you there?" his voice broke on the question and I watched him fall forward onto the bed, shoulders hunched and shaking. His sobs were silent and I could feel fresh tears slide down my own cheeks. I stepped out of the room leaving the door open and took up the post on the opposite side from Gideon. We stood as silent sentries to the brother's grief.

When Aiden stepped from the room his eyes were still red from his tears and I could see the tear tracks that ran down his cheeks. He straightened his shoulders as he pulled the door closed behind him, "Thank you for letting me see her. My parents wished for me to ask again for her to be returned home."

"No," Gideon's response was short, clipped, and nearly cold, "we aren't giving up on her yet. Once we find all the artifacts we will bring her back." Aiden looked at Gideon, shoulders and back stiff. After a moment he gave one short nod.

"In that case, I need to see the Altar. I need to see where the portals are to be set up."

"Gideon, I can show him where it is if you want to reseal the door and go down with the others." His only response was to turn and place his palm against the heavy wood of the door. I nodded my head towards the stairs, "this way." I told Aiden. We climbed the two sets of stairs that lead past the third floor and to the attic landing in silence and when we reached the landing I opened the door and showed him in. I let him walk around the rug, studying the altar.

"There is a magic circle here."

"It's woven into the rug and amplified by the lay lines that run under the house. One of the others downstairs made it," I tapped on the wall to my right softly, "Kenna has already labeled where each Portal should be."

Aiden shook his head with a soft laugh and made his way to one of the walls. He reached up tracing his sister's handwriting with a finger, "of course she did." He turned to look at me and set his bag down on the floor, "It'll take me a few hours to get these all set up. Do you have to stay and watch?"

"I don't think the others will allow me to leave you here alone, but I can sit just outside the door to give you privacy as I did downstairs."

"I would appreciate that, thank you." I nodded to him and stepped out of the room. I slid down the wall just to the left of the door and closed my eyes head tipped back and one leg stretched out in front of me. I could hear a soft chanting start inside the room and feel just the faintest hum of magic. I lost track of time letting myself sink into oblivion.

"You ok seer?" I opened my eyes and looked up into Alec's eyes as he stood over me.

I nodded, "tired, and thinking."

"How's it going in there and why are you out here?"

"Aiden asked for some privacy," I shrugged my shoulders, "I figure this can't be easy for him, and having some stranger breathing down his neck won't help."

"He looks like her," his voice was softer, quieter.

"I know," I laughed a little, "when he stepped out of the car I nearly lost it." Alec reached a hand down to me and I took it with a smile. He pulled me to my feet and I slid an arm around his waist. I leaned into him, letting myself gain what minute comfort I could from him. "We should check on him." I tilted my chin towards the door.

"In a minute" Alec's voice was a soft rumble as he pulled me tighter and tilted his head, so our cheeks rested against each other.

I turned and pressed our lips together softly, "I think I'm starting to fall in love with you, Soldier Boy" I whispered and closed my eyes as his hands tightened against me.

"I know I am." His voice was just as quiet as mine had been and my breath caught in my throat, "come on seer, let's go check on our guest." We turned pulling away from each other and headed into the room. As soon as we stepped into the room I could feel that the energy in the room had boosted significantly over the last few hours.

Aiden stood in front of the wall just to the right of the door. He held his hands out in front of him, eyes closed, and mouth moving in a silent chant. I watched as the garnets now embedded in the worn wood of the altar pulsed. I turned to see a small swirl of purple start in the center of the wall and slowly grow larger until it was big enough for two people to walk through comfortably. When he dropped his hands the portal closed but the hum of magic that had started when it opened was still there. He opened his eyes and looked over at us. I could see the exhaustion in his eyes even before he stumbled back a step. Alec stepped forward and caught him with an arm around his waist. I joined him on Aiden's other side and we moved him over to one of the wing-backed chairs that someone had added to the room.

"You ok?" I asked as Alec guided his head down between his knees.

"I didn't know it would take so much out of me." His voice was raspy.

"Well it did and now you need to get it back," Alec pointed out. He looked up at me, "I am going to go and grab

Gwen. See if there is anything she can do to help." I nodded as I moved to kneel in front of Aiden.

"You should have stopped when you realized it was draining this much out of you," I chided him.

"I needed to get them all set up," he wouldn't meet my eyes, "I'm just not used to working this much magic alone. Kenna was always there with me when we had to learn to do anything complex."

"I understand but you can't rely on her right now and you can't help us get her back if you are dead."

"You really think we can get her back?"

I shrugged, "Gideon is determined. And from what I have learned about him he doesn't fail."

"She mentioned him to me," he turned to look at me, "Gideon, I think she was falling in love with him. Does he love her? Did he treat her right? Did he even try to protect her?" his voice had gone hard and angry with the last question.

"I do love her, and I did try to protect her," Gideon answered from where he stood in the doorway with Alec and Gwen, "But she wouldn't let me. I tried to talk your sister out of going into the Astral Planes alone, but she wouldn't listen to me. She was determined to prove to your parents and everyone else that she could do this one thing, and it cost her her life. Now I will find a way to bring her back and when I do, I will make sure that she is never hurt again. I love your sister, and I know that she at the very minimum cared for me as well. I won't tell you that she loved me as it is not my place. I will however let her tell you that herself when I get her back." He turned his gaze away from Aiden to me, "Once you have him back on his feet Misty and Esme have dinner done." He turned on his heels and walked away as Gwen stepped to the door a small bag in her hand.

"What am I going to do with you all?" she demanded as she nudged me out of the way, "What must I do to make you all understand that until the arti-facts are back our inner power is di-minished? You cannot do spell work until you are faint from exhaustion." She lectured on as she began to take Aiden's blood pressure and give him a full check over. She sat back on her knees as she finished. "You should be fine Aiden, but you cannot perform any magic for at the very minimum of two days. I don't care how simple of a spell you think it is, or if you have your familiar plastered to your side, you cannot do it." She looked up into his exhausted face, eyes hard and didn't look away until he nodded his understanding. She nodded once and stood, "Good. You two can get him downstairs. A hot meal will help him immensely."

"We will get him downstairs," Alec said from where he stood by the door. We all watched Gwen leave the room.

"He thinks he can get her back." Aiden's voice was quiet and he was looking through the open door where the other two had disappeared.

"He believes that if we can get all the artifacts back, get all the powers back online, that we can save her," I answered him slowly. I still wasn't convinced that Gideon was right in his assumption but I also wasn't ready to discount it.

"Do you think he's right?" Now he turned his gaze on me, "Do you think we can save my sister?"

I sighed and looked down, gathering myself before I looked up to meet his gaze, "I don't know Aiden. I want to believe he is right, but everything we have read so far does not point to success."

"What one are you looking for?"

"The Amethyst Mirror, it's what holds the power of premonition. If we get it, it will make finding the rest a little easier," I stood and held a hand down to him, "Come on let's go ~~get~~ downstairs before Gwen comes back up for us."

He nodded and took my hand and together we pulled him to his feet. He swayed a little and Alec stepped forward and slid an arm around his waist to steady him, "Easy there." His deep voice was soft.

Aiden closed his eyes as if steadying himself. When he opened them again he looked at him, "Three flights down. This should be fun," he swallowed as we made our way to the door. "Zander can you distract me? Tell me how you are planning to find the mirror?" he was winded by the time we reached the top of the first flight of stairs.

"I can carry you if you want," Alec's offer was soft but Aiden shook his head.

"No, I can do this, it just will take some time. If we were going up the steps, then I might have taken you up on that offer." Alec nodded and we began the descent down.

I moved to go in front of Alec and Aiden going down the stairs sideways. I was almost backward so I could watch in case they needed help, "We have evidence that the mirror is in Rhode Island. We are working with a new group; they want to bring together a way for us all to help each other, Vampires, Elves, Witches, and Shifters. They were able to give us a nearly exact location. A few of us will be heading out in a few days once we get the last of the supplies that we need.

"A group that wants to bring all supernaturals together? The covens can't even come together, and you think a few people will be able to bring all the groups of supernaturals together?" I could hear the disbelief in his voice.

I laughed a little, "yeah, that's what I thought too, but they already started. There's an office in Las Vegas staffed with several members from all the groups. We want to start one here next." I looked into his eyes as we stopped to give him a break on the second landing. "Aiden if A-VEWS can get momentum with the covens, and then with the vampire houses, maybe we can get the shifter groups on board and then possibly even the elves. What we need is to show everyone that A-VEWS helps them. That's the whole point of A-VEWS, to help all the groups, to pool resources. Aiden, I need to ask for a favor, I need to ask you to take the information about A-VEWS back to your coven and talk to them about it. I need you to convince them that they should support the group. A-VEWS can help us find the artifacts, and if Gideon is right, the artifacts can get help us get Kenna back."

Aiden looked away and I could watch the thoughts race across his face. He turned back, eyes filled with determination, "I will do what I can and if you save my sister we will call it even."

"We need you to talk to them about one more thing," Alec said from next to him, "we need to find out who the other witches were. The Circle just outside of Vegas has agreed to look through their archives, and the rest of us are reaching out to those back home to see what they can find. We need to know if the Shadow Walker coven has any information at all."

Aiden nodded without hesitation, "Mom had already started looking through things when Kenna reported that other witches had stolen the altar. I'll talk to her and see what she knows and then start looking through things myself."

"Thank you," Alec said and with that, we all continued down the stairs.

CHAPTER 17

THE NEXT MORNING WE gathered everyone around the kitchen table after breakfast. Gideon and Jamal were the only ones missing as they had left a few hours previously to take Aiden back to the airport. As they left they had given us permission to find possible locations for the bar that would stand as the front for this branch of A-VEWS. We had spread an enlarged map of New Orleans over the old worn table. We had found some multi colored dot stickers in a box in the basement and now a hand full of them were scattered across the map. We marked each available space as Eris read off addresses as she found them on her laptop.

"It should be somewhere close to the downtown area but probably not in the French Quarter," Eliza, "That leaves us with these three locations." She said tapping the dots.

"There's an awesome little meta-physics shop next to this one here," Misty said tapping one, "Remember it, Esme? They had all those fresh herbs drying in the front window."

She nodded, "Oh yeah, they said they grew them on the roof or some-thing like that."

"This one is pretty close to the house," Eris said as she walked over to join us at the table.

Randall stood against the wall arms crossed, "How close do we really want this to be? I understand that the point of A-VEWS is for all of us to work to-gether, but I don't think we should be advertising where the Artifacts will be being kept once we have them all back." We all looked up at him.

"Right," Eris used a nail to pick the dot off the location less than two blocks from the house, "Let's take this one out of the running."

"That leaves just the other two lo-cations," Gwen looked over at Eliza, "I think we would all vote to locate next to the herbal shop, but what about you. Would it be better to be farther away from anything that could be considered supernatural?"

Eliza drummed her fingers on the table as she chewed on her lip thoughtfully, "I'm honestly not sure. Let me reach out to Lana and see what she says."

We all nodded our agreement, "Speaking of the herbal shop," I looked over at the girls, "I need to go grab a few things from there. I want to have the supplies for a few different potion options before we head to Rhode Island."

"While you three go do that, a couple of us can go check out the other location," Jamal said.

"Sounds like a plan," Esme winked.

***

Misty had been accurate in her description of the shop. The windows in the front of the shop were lined with bundles of herbs that had been hung up to dry. Under them was a collection of crystals that caught the sunlight and glimmered. When I opened the door I traced my fingers over the strange pattern in the wood, it looked as if the wood had once been marred by phantom claws. I made my way around the store's shelves that were filled with candles, tarot and oracle cards, basket hooked over my arm. The heavy wooden shelves must have been crafted from the same tree as the door where I found more of the strange marks. I felt a shiver run up my back when I touched them. I added a couple of dozen small glass bottles to the basket before starting on the herbs. I filled the small bags that they had with Acacia, Bluebell, Calamus, and several more. By the time I made my way up to the counter the basket was heavy enough that the handles dug into my arm.

"And what are we making with all this?" the older woman behind the counter asked as she began to ring up the items.

I flashed her the grin I had perfected for spectators on the strip, "oh you know just a little of this, a little of that."

"A crafty one are you?"

I laughed and winked, "when the situation calls for it." I saw her cheeks brighten with just a touch of pink and felt my grin widen.

"Will you stop teasing the poor lady?" Misty said bumping me aside with her hip.

"I wasn't teasing I was conversing," I handed the cashier my card and took it back with another wink as I grabbed my herb ladened bags.

I stood to the side as Misty began to check out, "I apologize for him. I swear we house broke him but the training just doesn't seem to stick." She smiled at the now only slightly flustered cashier.

"Oh, no worries he was fine." I had to bite back a laugh at the double entendre.

"Yes, he is, sadly he is also taken by a beefy Marine."

The cashier's eyes widened just a touch, "oh you mean he's, um," the sentence trailed off.

"Yeah," Misty nodded with a sigh, "I know it disappointed a lot of us."

"Now why did you have to ruin my fun?" I asked as we both walked out of the store into the darkening dusk.

"Because you don't need to be leading that poor lady on, and if Alec had been with he probably would have given her a heart attack."

"Oh, he's not that intimidating," I tried to ignore the flair of arousal as I flashed back to him pinning me to the hallway wall.

"Yeah ok, I heard your squeak of fear when he shoved you against the wall outside my room the other night.

My face felt like it was on fire suddenly and I looked at her, "please tell me you are the only one who heard us."

She shook her head with a grin, "oh no, Esme and I were up most of the night speculating on what you two getting up to in there, on that one very small bed."

Fuck I thought, "Let's take a look at this place." I said changing the subject and nodded my head towards the empty building when Esme walked out of the store, her own bag in hand.

Misty laughed, "Changing the subject much?"

"You bet," I muttered. I peeked through the dusty windows to peer at the interior. I could see tables that had been knocked over, and chairs randomly scattered. It looked like there was an old cracked mirror behind the old bar.

From what we could see through the windows the place had the potential and around the back of the building we had found an old rickety set of stairs that let to what seemed to be apartments above the bar. We all agreed that the upstairs would make a could headquarters for A-VEWS with the bar below for cover.

***

About an hour after we had first entered the store we were making our way towards the second location where the others were at. The now-empty bar seemed to need quite a bit of work on the inside from what we could see through the windows.

The three of us couldn't decide if that was a good thing or not. We were about a block from the others when two figures stepped out in front of us. Without a thought, all three of us dropped our bags to the sidewalk and pulled our daggers from where we had hidden them.

"What are you doing in our town?" one of the figures asked, the voice thick with the southern accent the natives of New Orleans seamed to have. They stood just far enough out of reach from the glow of the closest streetlight that their faces were shadowed.

"Your town?"

"Yes, our town. The Vampires have held control of New Orleans since the 1700's now you witches have shown up and have brought death with you."

"We are not here to cause trouble for the vampires," I said stepping in front of the other two and tucking my blade back into the sheath at the small of my back. I held my hands out to show them that I was unarmed.

"Yet you come here, your house smells of looming death and within weeks of your appearance we are no longer able to contact our Lords."

"We did not cause that. I am friends with a Vampire from the House of Aquarius, she mentioned that no one has been able to reach anyone at the House of Ophiuchus. We want to help. We are looking for artifacts that were stolen from the witches. Once we have the needed artifact back I will be able to help you. I am a seer, I was raised in the circle and I have been able to call up prophecies and visions for as long as I can remember. But right now, until we get the artifact back, I am at the mercy of the fates and what they decide to show me. Once we have our powers back I will help you find out what is happening to your people myself."

"Vampires are not friends with spell weavers." The second one hissed.

"I am friends with a vampire. I also have a friend who is a shifter. I have nothing to gain in the long term by lying to you. Call the House of Aquarius, ask them about Lana Mae, and ask them about A-VEWS. We only want to help." They leaned their heads together and whispered to each other.

The first one nodded, "We will give you passage today. If we have not received help from you within the next moon cycle we will remove you from our territory permanently." They turned and melted back into the shadows where they had previously been hiding, and I let out a breath.

"You ever thought of going into politics?" Esme asked as she and Misty joined me, handing me back my dropped bags.

"Nope, I enjoy my privacy, and most politicians still don't like the gays."

"Let's get back to the others," Misty said her voice filled with an edge of fear and I noticed she was still gripping her dagger. I nodded and we all started back to find the others.

CHAPTER 18

I STOOD IN FRONT of the bed looking down at everything that was laid out and leaned back against Alec when he squeezed my shoulders. I had gone through everything twice. I had triple-checked the recipes for the potions I wanted to make once we were in Rhode Island, and spent an hour on the phone with my sister while she passed along everything the coven had learned. Unfortunately, that wasn't much.

"You have done everything you can. Relax until morning when we leave." He pressed a kiss to my temple and I leaned my face against his.

"I'm trying. I just," I sighed and closed my eyes as he wrapped his arms around me, "I have a bad feeling about this. Like we are missing some vital information."

"Whatever it is we will deal with it when it comes up. You aren't alone anymore."

"Gwen mentioned that they had the boards set up downstairs. I was thinking before we leave maybe we work with the others to get that filled in. Then we can get Eliza to start setting up searches for those things like they did with the mirror."

I felt his chest rumble against my back as he laughed, "don't you ever just rest?"

"We don't have the time to waste. Not if we want to have any hope of saving Kenna."

He turned me to face him, "Zander, you have to know that the chances of us bringing her back are slim. And that the attempt to do so is dangerous." His eyes searched mine.

I lifted my hand to cup his cheek, "Alec, I know there is very little chance, and yes I know that the road to do so won't be easy. But, if you were in Gideon's position and I was the one not quite dead wouldn't you do everything in your power to bring me back to you?"

He sighed and touched his brow to mine, "Of course I would, I love you." My chest squeezed at his words and I turned to him as I pressed my lips to his.

"I love you too," my words were whispered against his mouth, "now let's go interview the others." I slid my hand down his arms as I stepped back and took his hand in mine.

We walked out of the room and stood in the small hallway, "How exactly were you planning on getting everyone's attention?" He looked down at me lifting an eyebrow.

"Well you were a drill instructor weren't you?" I grinned.

He laughed and shook his head, "No but I knew enough of them." I watched him stand just the slightest bit straighter and pull in a deep breath, his chest expanding. He placed his fingers to his mouth and let out a whistle so loud and high pitched that I had to cover my ears. When the other began to rush out of rooms and through the stair ways I had to laugh.

"What the hell?" Ade demanded from her and Eris's doorway.

"Sorry guys, but I didn't know any other way to get everyone's attention," I had to wipe away tears as I tried to calm my laughing. "I wanted to talk to everyone about sitting down with each of you and gathering some info. We mentioned the other day that we need to compile what everyone was looking for and I think we should do it before we leave again. We just need get on the same page then maybe we can get things done smoother. If all of us know everything, and not just bits and pieces it will help."

Ed nearly rolled his eyes as he turned to head back downstairs, "You have all my information, so I am going to go back to watching the game."

"Do we really have to do this? It seems like a waste of time," Eris scoffed. I watched Ade give her shoulder a nudge and she rolled her eyes, "I mean if we really have to then let's get it over with." The interaction made me raise an eyebrow at the sassy Chicagoan who only smirked back at me.

"Since you seem so excited to get this done I can get your information first Eris." I smiled at the blonde. Every now and then I could see a softer side to her but she seemed to keep it guarded under her cold façade.

***

It took me about three hours to go through everyone. I decided to record it all in my notebook where I had the notes from the drive to Vegas instead of immediately putting it all up on the board. I ended up taking time to talk more with Randall and Ed to get information to pass onto Eliza to plug into the A-VEWS data basis. It took me another hour to put it all on the board that had been set up, and shot an email off to Eliza to flagging things that would signal different artifacts. By the time I had finished everything, the girls, with Jamal's help, had finished dinner. Alec promptly plucked the notebook out of my hands and escorted me, semi forcefully, to join the others to eat.

"Zander are you ok?" Ade asked from where she sat across from me.

I looked up as her words pulled me from my thoughts, "Huh? Yeah, I'm fine Ade." I sent her a smile.

"You look exhausted. I know that we are all anxious to find the artifacts, but you are putting in a lot of time and effort. You need to make sure you get the rest you need. If you come up against more of the Witches like we did in New Hampshire or another elf like Kenna, you need to be in top shape. You can't help Kenna if you are lying dead next to her."

"She's right," Gideon said from where he sat next to Ade and I wondered if I looked as beat as he did. His once youthful face was drawn and his eyes sat above dark circles. When he tried to smile at me it was only a half-smile that never reached his eyes.

I reached across the table and set my hand over his, "We are gonna get her back." I squeezed his hand and he again sent me one of the half smiles.

***

After dinner, I headed back to what we decided to refer to as the War Room and worked to hook up a TV to the computer with a map of the US on it. I wanted to set up a system with Eliza that would show a live update of all suspicious activity A-VEWS found.

"You're right, I think this will help more than anything else we have thought of," Eris said as she leaned against the door frame, "I can work on making sure that map stays up to date."

I looked over my shoulder at her, "I would like to work with A-VEWS to have it stay update live, but it would be helpful if you could do it manually until then. I set up an email address for us while I was in Vegas, I can get you that information and will have them send everything there."

"I think we can work something out. The others were right at dinner though, you look like shit," I laughed and rolled my eyes. Same old Eris, "no really. If you are planning on being of any help tomorrow, you need to go get some sleep."

I thought over what she said and nodded, "Yeah, I guess you're right. I flipped off the light as I walked out of the room. I stopped and put a hand on her shoulder, "I don't know what it is you are going through Eris, but I think you need to decide now if you are going to be one of us or not. Ade's a good person, and I think she will vouch for you with the others, but you need to decide if you want them to like and trust you or not." I gave her shoulders a soft squeeze and then headed up the stairs to join Alec in sleep.

CHAPTER 19

I TOSSED MY BAG into the back of the van and stepped back for the three familiars to jump inside. Gwen came out of the house with a large black bag in hand and walked over to where we stood.

"I put this together for you boys. It is a bunch of simple first aid remedies just in case something happens like with Gideon and the fire ball."

"You are a worry wart," Randall said as he took the bag from her.

"No, I am practical and am the one who has to put you all back together when you try to kill yourselves doing something foolish. You think I don't know what its like when boys go off with out a woman to tell them not to do the stupid thing?" she fisted a hand on her hip and staired at us. I looked down and scuffed my shoes against the cement, I felt like a school boy being scolded by the teacher.

"We will behave," Alec said setting a comforting hand on her shoulder and giving it a squeeze, "you don't worry while we are gone and just focus on stuff here."

"I will be doing both," she huffed slightly.

We all moved around the vehicle and were getting in when Ade ran out of the house, "don't go pulling away yet." She yelled before we could even close our doors. "You guys can't go straight to Rhode Island," she huffed grabbing the side door to keep it open, "you need to stop back in Salem. Go through the archives there and see what you can find about the witch trials. I just got off the phone with someone back home, I don't know anything concrete, as they wouldn't say anything over the phone, but they said that the answers about the witches lay in the trials. I am hoping that they mean the Salem Trials and not some convoluted trials we all have to go through."

"I never thought of looking at Salem," Ed said as we all looked at each other.

We all contemplated for a few moments, I set my hand on Ade's shoulder and gave it a squeeze, "thanks for the heads up. We will look into things at Salem, you just take care of everyone here, especially Gideon." I lowered my voice with the last.

She nodded and put her hand over mine giving it a squeeze, "don't ya'll go getting yourselves killed. It will seriously piss me off to lose anyone else." I laughed and leaned out of the van to give her a quick hug. When she stepped back I closed the door and Randall pulled away from the street.

"If you guys are ok with it, I may be able to expedite this drive just a little," his gruff voice was quiet.

"What do you have in mind?" Alec asked from next to me.

"I have been trying to tap into the teleportation powers, and while I can't pop from one place to another, with a little concentration and a lot of power I can seem to bend things a little to get things moving."

"How badly will this wipe you out?" Ed asked worriedly.

"I can maybe do it once every other day, but it should cut the time I'm behind the wheel in half. I'll just have to pass out after."

"Call Tyr up by you and have him help you. Do about half of the max that you think you can do and then we will rotate driving. Don't go pushing yourself too much, we don't know what we are getting into." Alec said, and the command was back in his voice. I shifted as Randall called Tyr to him to let the large grey wolf pass and then settled into the seat. I tipped my head back just as the magic raised around us and the world outside the windows blurred.

When I woke we had already made it to Ashville, Alabama. We all clambered from the van and Alec moved to start pumping gas while the rest of us made our way inside the gas station. Once inside we all split off to commandeer our needed provisions. I grabbed an arm full of soda and water before heading to the snack aisle to grab several bags of the salt and vinegar chips that Alec despised but I loved. My last stop before heading to the register was the small open refrigerated section to grab jerky, fruits and vegetables for Alec. I had just gotten into line when he stepped inside. I lifted my head to signal him over.
"Doing all the shopping now?" he grinned.
"Bite me." I rolled my eyes as he began taking the items I had grabbed for him and grinned when he grimaced at the sight of the chips.

"Not if you plan on eating any of those." He grouched. I laughed and touched my head to his arm. It took us less than twenty minutes to all get through the line and back on the road, this time with me in the passenger seat, Alec driving, and the others in the back. Within minutes of being on the road Randall was asleep against the window, Tyr curled up tightly around his feet.

***

Alec got us to just outside of Washington D.C. when we decided to pull into a motel and get a few rooms for the night. Once the van was unloaded and we were in our rooms I sent Ade a quick message to let her know we were bedding down for the night and where we were. I leaned back into Alec's arms when he stepped up behind me, tilting my head to the side to give him full access to my throat and was about to toss my phone to the side when it rang. I nearly growled, and wanted to even more when I saw my sisters name on the screen.

"Have I ever told you that you have horrible timing?" I answered.

"You'll live, tell Mr. Muscles hello from me," she said, "Are you guys on your way to Rhode Island yet? Lana and I have some information but I think it would be best if we give it to you in person."

"You are leaving the state? How did you manage that?"

"I'll tell you that story when I see you. Now are you on your way to Rhode Island or not?"

"We are on our way there now, it'll probably be about two days though, since we are stopping in Salem tomorrow."

"What's in Salem?"

"Hopefully answers." I closed my eyes to concentrate on the conversation as Alec began softly biting at my throat and shoulder.

"If you guys are looking at the trials, then look for Goody Proctor in the archives. We keep seeing mention of her in old coven journals but I can't seem to find anything concrete."

"Is that what you need to tell us about?"

"That and more. I'll explain when I see you. I will try to be on the ground when you guys get there but traveling cross country with a Vampire isn't easy."

"Has she heard anything else about the House of Ophiuchus?"

"No but we think that that's part of the information we have. Just wait till Rhode Island. I'll tell you where we are landing and when as soon as I have the details." She hung up before I could respond.

"What was that about?" Alec whispered into my ear causing my to shiver.

"Apparently Lana and my sister have information. They are meeting us in Rhode Island."

"Why couldn't they just tell you over the phone?"

"I don't know, but she did give me a name for us to research tomorrow, Goody Proctor." I tossed the phone and turned to face him, "Now lets forget about my sister and Lana for the night." I ordered before sealing our mouths together.

Chapter 20

THE MORNING CAME FASTER than I liked and wondered how I had managed to surround myself with morning people. Even as I glared at Alec he grinned back as he let Randall and Ed into the room with their gift of coffee and breakfast sandwiches. While I splashed my face with cold water to try to force the wake up Alec tossed the clothes from the night before into our duffle bags as he chatted with the other two.

"Ready?" Alec asked softly stepping up behind me at the sink when the others headed out to load their room into the van.

"For sleep," I grumbled as I dropped my tooth brush into the small toiletry bag of mine on the sink.

"You can sleep in the car, I have me and you on the night shift," he turned me to face him and kissed me soft, "You seem to do better at night." Taking my hand he pulled me out of the small bathroom area, grabbing my toiletry bag as he did. He tossed it into my duffle and zipped it closed before handing it to me. He kept my hand in his as he picked up his own duffle before pulling me from the room. It wasn't until we were climbing into the car that I noticed he had tucked Dazzle into his own shirt pocket. I smiled up at him as I plucked the chameleon from his shirt and set him on my shoulder. As I cuddled into Alec's side, Dazzle cuddled Into my neck. If I didn't know any better, I would have sworn that he yawned in exhaustion as Ed pulled out of the parking lot.

***

By the time we pulled into Salem the next night all official buildings had already closed for the night, so we decided to head straight for a hotel that Alec had found for us while I drove the final leg of the trip. I sat on the bed, back resting against the headboard and watched Dazzle explore the dresser and mirror in his normal slow pace.

"You ok?" Alec asked as he slid onto the bed next to me.

"Yeah, I just," I sighed and let my head fall back eyes closing, "I don't know Alec. I feel like we are missing something with all of this. Something that is right in front of us, and this feeling keeps getting stronger the farther north we go."

"Like what?"

"I don't know, but I feel like whatever it is, it's gonna come back to bite us all in the ass."

"If that happens, we will handle it, we always do." He snaked his arms around me and pulled me into his side. I let my head fall to his shoulder and closed my eyes, sinking into the safety of him. I force the feeling of impending doom away and instead focused on the comfort he offered.

***

The next morning I woke to the sun filtering through the curtains. I grumbled and buried my head into the pillow.

"Hey now, none of that, we gotta get moving." Alec said and I could hear the grin in his voice.

"Coffee," I groaned. Waking up with the sun for the third day in a row was slowly killing me, and I knew that if I didn't get a cup of the magical elixir I would soon be killing my cohorts.

"Get up and get ready then you can have coffee," he jerked the covers off the bed.

I rolled over and glared at him, "You are a sadist,"

He laughed and pulled me to the bottom of the bed where he stood by my ankle, pulling a yelp from me. When he palmed the front of my boxers my head fell back with a groan. He leaned down over me, mouth brushing against my ear as he whispered, "no darlin. I just enjoy seeing you all needy in the mornings." I nearly screamed when he stood up straight and walked away.

I reached above my head and grabbed a pillow before throwing it at his back, "ass." He laughed even as the pillow hit him square in the back of the head. With one last groan I rolled off the bed and landed on my feet before heading to the shower.

***

Several hours later I rubbed my tired eyes. We had been pouring over articles at the library looking for any mention of Proctor, or any hint we could find that she existed. After reading yet another account of one of the executions I reached across the table and took Alec's hand in mine. Just reading through them was sending ominous chills up my spine and adding to the bad feeling that had been plaguing me.

"You ok?" he asked deep voice soft in the quiet library.

"No. What these people went through, what our ancestors went through, " I shook my head, unable to voice the rage and terror I felt.

He squeezed my hand, "I know." He stood and walked around to the same side of the table I was sitting on. Bringing the records he was looking through with him, he sat next to me. He pulled on my arm and settled me against his side, turning me so my back pressed into him. He held me against him with an arm across my chest and we both went back to reading. Somehow being close to him help to calm the emotions storming through me.

***

Less than an hour later I hit gold. I spun back to the table pulling Alec's attention away from what he was reading, "What did you find?" He closed his book and looked over my shoulder at the text.

"The old arrest records. Here they took away and arrested Proctor but she isn't in the execution list and I can't find her name after this. It's like after her arrest she disappeared."

"When did that happen?"

I scanned through the pages until I could find a date, "It looks like it happened in early August." I looked up at him, "Do you know when the covens decided to seal off the powers?"

He shook his head, "No, I will shoot off a text to the others and see if they cant find out." He pulled his phone from his pocket and quickly send off the message, causing my own phone to vibrate in my pocket. When he looked back up at me I could see a fire in his eyes, "Let's see what else we can find."

***

Alec and I met up with the others for lunch, hauling our note with us. We found a corner booth and began comparing notes. We told them what we had found, or more accurately not found past the arrest record, and they relayed the list of arrests and executions they had gotten from the city archives, with the accompanying accusations. There wasn't nearly as much as I had hoped to glean from the old records.

"I want to go back to the clearing," I said looking up at the others, "If there is anywhere that I can draw power from around here it would be there."

"What are you hoping to do that you need a boost of power?" Ed asked.

"A few readings. I just have this feeling, and I can't seem to shake it. I want to see if the cards or runes will tell me anything," I shrugged, "maybe the fates or the ancestors will talk to me more freely there."

"You are gonna do both?" I could hear the concern in Alec's voice and reached out to pat his hand.

"I am, and I will be fine. I have been reading since before I could actually read. It's like breathing for me."

"Just be careful," Randall said, "I'm not fully drained from the trip up here but I'm also not at one hundred percent. We don't need two of us compromised."

"Readings don't drain me," I smiled a little, "dream premonitions on the other hand." I shrugged, "and I can't promise not to have one of them. I can't control those." The others all nodded in understanding.

"When are we leaving?" Alec asked. I looked at him and I'm sure my confusion showed in my face, "You are not going out there alone."

"I also can't afford any distractions. I am a big boy Alec; I can take care of myself."

"I never said you couldn't, but we are up against dangerous people. They have already killed twelve other witches in that exact location, so no I am not allowing you to go there alone. I will stay at the edges, but I will not allow you to put yourself in possible danger."

I wanted to argue but I could tell we had started to draw the attention of outsiders, "Fine." I nearly snarled.

***

We took a cab to the edge of the forest where the clearing was located and tipped the driver. I adjusted my backpack as we headed into the woods and I was over come with Déjà vu. As we moved silently through the trees all I could think was the last time I had made this trip so late in the evening I had found twelve dead and eleven strangers waiting for me. By the time we reached the clearing the sky overhead was a deep purple, and growing darker by the second. I could still faintly see where the grass hadn't fully grown back over where we had buried the Elders. Just as he promised Alec stopped just at the edge of the clearing and settled himself down leaning back against a tree. I moved to the exact center of the clearing, careful to walk around the outlines of the graves, and there I could feel a soft buzz around me. I knelt down and opened my backpack. I took out the purple satin cloth and set it in front of me. Next were several small tealight candles inside the small glass cups that held them and would protect the flames from the wind. Using my phone I found due north and set out the green candle. Moving clockwise I placed yellow, red, and blue to form a rough circle. Laying out the satin square I weighed it down with the last four candles, black in the top left, white in the top right and then two purple at the bottom corners. Finally, I pulled out the bag holding my cards and the bag holding the runes. Lastly, I grabbed the box of matches before setting my bag outside the circle.

I lit the candles in the same order I had laid them out, calling on the four corners and then on the god and goddess to boost my reading. I took out the cards first and closed my eyes, allowing the movement of shuffling them to calm and center me. Feeling grounded I began to lay out the cards, letting them fall where they felt natural. When I set down the last card, I felt my blood go cold. Four cards, four of cups reversed, Death in the upright, three of cups reversed, and the five of sword upright. Letting out a breath I gathered the cards and tucked them back into the bag pulling the strings tight.

I set the bag aside and picked up the bag that rattled with the stones inside. I reached into the bag and let the cool Amethyst stones roll around my fingers as I mixed them. Cupping my fingers, I scooped out what ever stayed in my hand, then dumped them onto the satin. There it was again. The first one I saw was laguz, the water rune, the second was algiz which was in the transverse direction. Death. I didn't need to look at the other two stones, there was no denying it anymore. Someone would die in the retrieving of the mirror, and water would be the weapon that killed them. I gathered up the stones and placed them back in the bag. Giving a soft thank you I extinguished the candles and grabbed the flashlight from my bag to use as I cleaned up.

When I had finished, I walked over to where Alec watched me with concerned eyes. I just shook my head and took his hand when he stood. Together we made our way back to the road where we would call another cab to take us back to the hotel.

Chapter 21

WE WERE BACK ON the road before the sun had fully breached the horizon the next day and headed towards Rhode Island. I hadn't slept the entire night, and the exhaustion was weighing on me, not to mention the knowledge I had yet to share with the others. How could I tell them, that another of us would soon be dead. We were about thirty minutes in when Alec squeezed my hand and I turned from the window to look at him.

"What's going on Zander?" he kept his voice quiet.

I took a deep breath, I guess now was as good a time as any. "We are going to Rhode Island to deal with homicidal witches. Every reading I have done in the last two months since the Artifacts have been stolen has alluded to death. The last premonition I had not only alluded to death but to water, and we are going to Rhode Island, which has a lot of water around it. To top it off the last several readings I have done have also called out both water and Death."

"Now I feel like there is something that I am missing," I could see the concern in his eyes,

I let myself lean against him and sighed. He wasn't catching onto the fact that someone would die and I couldn't bring myself to say it outright. So instead I told him the other truth, "I am terrified of boats. It's not the water so much, but boats in and of themselves. I am from the desert; boats don't make sense to me and they terrify me. And I know that there is this huge probability that I am going to end up on a flipping boat." The last sentence was a whispered yell and I could feel my ire rise when I felt his chest shake in a laugh. I glared up at him, "are you laughing at me?"

He cleared his throat but couldn't hide his grin, "I am not meaning to laugh at you. But Zander, even if we do have to get on a boat, the waters that we will be in? There is very little chance that anything will happen to the boat. Even if something did, we will be in waters that we could easily swim."

I sat up and crossed my arms, "That is not the point Alec. I understand that logically there is nothing to be afraid of but that doesn't negate the fact that I am afraid. Isn't there anything that you are scared of?"

He reached over and cupped my chin in his hand and looked directly into my eyes, "losing you." His voice was soft and serious now and I felt my heart melt. I leaned back into him and pressed my lips to his, hoping I could convey my feelings as I couldn't seem to find the words to do so.

"That's enough you two," growled Randall from the front seat, "besides we are here."

"And where is here exactly?" Alec asked pulling me in against his side.

"Warwick, it's one of the towns on the list that has been repeated a few times so it seemed like a good bet." Ed shrugged.

"I'll message Kat and let her know. We should get an extra room for her and Lana," I pull out my phone and send off a quick message with our location and hotel.

"I'll run in and get the rooms while you talk to her," Alec said sliding to the door, "then maybe we should head out around the town and see what we can find."

"Sounds like a plan," Randall answered.

***

Within the hour we had split in two and were canvasing the area. Kat had messaged that she expected to be in town just after sundown. They would fill us in with what they had found when we met up at the hotel.

"Let's stop in for a drink," Alec said ducking his head toward a small pub.

"Seriously? a drink now?" I looked at him incredulously.

"You would be surprised by what you can learn listening to the town drunks," he grinned.

I shook my head grinning, "I will take your word for it."

The building was dimly lit and the bar Alec sat us at was sticky. I had to fight not to grimace. I lost that battle when Alec ordered two beers, I hated the taste. When I gave him a look he just grinned, "You have to learn to blend Seer." I just rolled my eyes before glaring down at the amber colored liquid.

"I heard that they will be back in three days, but who knows. They never seem to give real notice," I heard in a deep voice behind me just as I was about to take the first awful sip.

I set the glass back on the bar and turned to see two men in jeans and worn button up shirts sitting a little ways down the bar from us.

"I know, I wish they would though. By the time I get free from work the line is already past what they are willing to take for the day. Me and Jinny could really use a break though and I just know that those three could help." The one farther from me said, his voice a rough smoker's voice.

I looked at Zander and lifted an eyebrow, tilting my head toward the two men.

"Wait and see." he mouthed, but I could tell he too was intrigued.

"Did you hear about how Max and Rita found her mama's old diamond in a jewelry box in the attic? they got enough money selling that off that they kept the house." The first man said.

"They told Jeff where his old crazy grandpa buried all that cash on his farm too."

I looked at Alec and with a soft sigh he nodded. smirking, I stood and approached the two men with an easy smile plastered on my face, "I'm sorry to intrude, but I'm new in town and I just couldn't help overhearing you. May I ask what exactly you are talking about?" The two men looked at each other then at me.

"The sisters." the closer man said.

"They started coming around about a month ago. They seem to be able to help everyone in just the way that they need most. They told my sister that she needed to go see her Doctor immediately. When she did it turned out she had some rare disease that had it not been caught now she most likely would have died from." His comrade said. I saw the first man nodding in eager agreement.

"I mean sure its not easy to come up with the fee but honestly its worth it most of the time." The first shrugged.

"And what is the fee?" I asked.

"Just about a hundred for a five-minute sitting, but if you really want the details needed it take a solid thirty minutes and that's a grand." He replied taking a drink of his beer.

I just stared. I couldn't believe this. They were scamming these people for everything they were worth, "And do you know where the sisters are located?"

The other gentleman shook his head, "No they come into the harbor about every other week or so, but there is never a guarantee as to when they will be here."

"I see. Thank you so much." I smiled at them and then jerked my head to the door and headed that way knowing Alec would follow.

"I take it you learned something?" He asked as we made our way back to the hotel.

"Yeah, that they are scamming the locals." I seethed, "I will fill you in when we have everyone, I don't know if can stomach saying it twice." I glanced up at the darkening sky, "Besides Lana and Kat should be here soon."

Chapter 22

I PACED THE SMALL hotel room while the other three watched me and waited for the knock on the door. Ever since we had left the bar I could feel a low simmer of anger that was on the edge of boiling over. Less than five minutes past full dark the knock came. I rushed to the door and opened it to the two women.

"What's going on Z?" Kat asked, and I knew she could see the rage in my eyes.

"We learned something about who has the mirror. Geeze Kat it goes against everything we were ever taught." I ran a hand through my hair, tugging at it and forcing myself to take a calming breath.

"Tell us what you learned first and then I will tell you what we know." She said sitting on the edge of the dresser.

"The other witches, the ones who have the mirror, are traveling to the coastal towns; I mean I assume that this isn't the only one they are going to based on the information that Eliza gained. They set up a booth and tell peoples fortunes. Things like they have a life altering medical condition, or where to find the lost family treasure. Hell they even just tell you what team to bet on. Here's the catch, if you want any real details that they claim to need thirty minutes with you."

"That's not how premonitions work," Katia's brow furrowed in confusion, "You get everything in just a few seconds, at most a minute. It may take a few minutes for a novice to comprehend and figure out how to voice what they saw, but no where near that long."

"I know. They will give you vague information in a five-minute sitting, if you only have the hundred they charge for that. However, they won't give you anything useful if you don't do the thirty-minute sit for a grand." I could hear the growl in my own voice as the barely tempered fury tried to rise again.

"That's ridiculous. They must be bleeding these people dry." Ed said, voice filled with disgust.

"What are we going to do?" Lana asked.

"We are going to find them, take back the mirror and stop them."

Kat smirked at me from where she sat in front of Lana, "Mad Scientist time?"

I laughed and grinned back, "Mad Scientist time."

***

It took less than an hour for Kat and me to transform Alec's and my hotel room into a potion's lab. The dresser had been cleared off and was now filled with an array of herbs in small bowls for easy access. The small table in the corner had a hot plate with a small kettle along with several tubes and beakers. The bathroom counter was filled with small bottles and their stoppers along with several small funnels.

"What all were you thinking for this one?" Kat asked.

"Simple, that way we can teach them, but I want to do a freezing potion along with a time slowing one"

"Alrighty then let's get started boys" she grinned as we turned to the others. After a few minutes we set up a second heating plate and I worked with Lana and Alec on the time delay potion while Kat taught Randal and Ed how to freeze time.

Before we had finished Lana retired to their room, and less than twenty minutes later the sky outside the windows was brightening. I slid the stopper into the last bottle just as the sun broke over the horizon, turning the curtained window burning glow and we all collapsed exhausted into seats and the bed.

"We still need to find where they are," Alec pointed out from where he was next to me.

"After a few hours of sleep" I groaned, resting my head on his muscled thighs. When his hand began to run through my shaggy hair I nearly dropped into unconsciousness then and there.

"Agreed," Randall said as he stood, "Everyone get a few hours of sleep and then we will look to see if we can find them

"Kat can you get into yours and Lana's room or do you wanna crash in here?" I yawned already turning my face into a pillow.

"I'll be good, Lana will have cocooned herself on the farthest bed." Our room emptied quickly and I let myself sink into both sleep and Alec's arms as they slid around me.

***

I groaned into the pillow when Alec shook me awake, "Come on sleepy head, time to get up. Ed just called, him and Randall are on their way with an early dinner."

"I hate you all" I growled and pulled the pillow over my head. A second later there was a loud crack and I yelped as I felt the sting in my ass. I sat up and turned to face Alec, "did you just spank me?"

He grinned, "It got you up."

"Ass" I laughed and threw the pillow at him. He growled and suddenly I was pinned back to the bed. I laughed again and leaned up fastening my lips to his. Just as I pushed up into him there was a knock at the door. Had Alec not slapped a hand over my mouth I would have told them to go away.

"Coming," Alec called and pulled me to my feet as he stood up. When he opened the door Ed and Randal came in ladened with takeout bags and rolled maps. Grumbling, I reached over for my phone to wake up Kat while they set everything out. When the scent of deep fried everything hit me I turned to see what they had gotten. Every container they opened was piled with brown shapes.

I looked up at the two men, "Haven't you ever heard of a vegetable?"

Ed held up one of the stir foam containers, "we have the deep fried broccoli right here." I just shook my head making a mental note to never send those two for dinner again.

***

Two hours later we had long finished eating and were busy arguing over where the witches were hiding.

"Why would they choose such a large island?" I asked when Kat insisted that they would be on Patience Island

"Why wouldn't they?" she challenged.

I shook my head, "They wouldn't want to be anywhere where people would want to go."

"So where do you think they are?"

"One of the smaller islands."

"Well that's helpful," she dragged her hand through her hair as she rolled her eyes. I couldn't help but meet her eye roll with one of my own and I drag the map of the bay closer so I can inspect it more thoroughly. I couldn't help but find it odd when every single island seemed to be labeled, even ones that seemed to be nothing more than a protruding rock. That's when I saw it. A tiny rock in the water labeled Despair Island,

"Here." I pointed and looked up at the other, "This is where they will go"

"Despair Island?" Ed read the name, "who the hell would name an island that?"

"I don't know, but this is where they are."

"Are you sure?" Alec looked at me and I nodded, "Ok, then we need to find a way to get us to Despair Island."

CHAPTER 23

KATIA WAS ABLE TO find a place not too far from us that offered boat tours of the bay. It showed them closed for the season, but when she called the number on the bottom of the website the owner agreed to take us out after Lana offered to pay almost three times his normal fee. We packed our bags, before all beginning to fill the small packs we would be bringing with us to the island. As we loaded up the two vans Lana headed to the front office to check us out of the three rooms we had needed.

"Think we should take both vehicles?" Kat asked, "I mean we could all fit into yours, even with the familiars. After we retrieve the mirror you can always just drop us back off here."

I looked at the others who just shrugged. Rolling my eyes I opened the back door and motioned my sister in. When Lana came back out she joined Kat and the three large familiars in the back row while I sat with Alec in the middle. It took us less than twenty minutes to get to the small shop and by the time Ed parked the van in the empty parking lot dread had filled every cell of my being. When we climbed from the van I could see the look of both confusion and exasperation on the old man's face when he stepped out of the building, "Which one of you are in charge of this circus?"

We all kind of looked at each other before we all looked at Randall who was the closest in age to the captain. With a grumble he walked forward, "I guess tonight that'd be me."

"Ya'll got permits for them critters?" he asked with a nod toward the three large animals, "Just want to make sure we have everything in order in case the wannabe water cops decide to stop us."

Randall gave a nod, "we got everything in needed to keep them with us." He said in a gruffer than usual voice.

"And the fee we discussed?" Lana stepped forward this time and handed him the bundle of bills. He gave them a quick ruffle as if to check the amount before nodding his head, "Right, well lets get going then," He turned and led us farther into the dark, toward the sound of water. When he led us to a small dock the feeling of unease doubled, and grew worse when I felt the dock bob under my foot. Had Alec not been behind me I would have aborted the mission and told the others I would wait in the van. Instead I forced myself to breath through the panic with every unsteady step. My resistance doubled down when the captain stepped into a boat that looked like it had been in the water longer than Randall had walked the earth.

I turned at looked at Alec who just shook his head and grinned at me, "You will be fine Seer." He whispered before helping me down into the already rocking boat with.
***

For the duration of the nearly thirty-minute ride to the island I sat in my spot in the small boat and clenched my eyes closed even as I fisted my hands on my lap. Every time a wave crashed against the side of the boat I had to swallow a yelp, instead forcing myself to take deep breaths of the salty air. I vowed to myself that once I was back on dry land I would never set foot in another one of these death traps no mater the reason.

"Are you ok?" Alec's voice whispered in my ear. All I could do was shake my head. When the boat shook as if it hit something I just barely contained the scream, a hand reaching out to grip his leg. "Hey easy, we just reached the shore, come on let's get you out, we are going to send the boat back out until we signal them." I let him help me to my feet and out of the boat to stumble onto the shore where I instantly felt better.

I paced a small section of land to steady my nerves and my legs, the gravel under foot crunching softly with every step. After a few steps I looked at Alec, "Once we are back on the main land, I am never getting into one of those death traps again."

He laughed and pulled me into a hug, "That wasn't even a rough ride Seer."

I growled into his chest, "Never again." He chuckled again before dropping a kiss to the top of my head. When I heard Lana tell the boat captain that we would signal him with the flare he gave her when we needed him to come back for us, I turned to look at the others. Once the boat was heading away from the island and back toward the main land, we all turned on the flashlights we had stowed in our bags and began searching.

We didn't have to look far, in the very center of the tiny rock of an island was a large multi room tent. "Looks like you called it," Ed said as we all approached the tent.

"Think they are in there?" Kat asked, her voice barely above a whisper.

"If they are then they know we are here." Randall pointed out. We all moved to surround the tent just in case. I crouched by the zippered door with Alec at my back. As I opened it, I slid off to the side holding my breath. When nothing happened, I ducked into the tent. And there on a small metal folding table was the Amethyst Mirror.

"Guys its here." I said as I walked hunched over to the table. I hit a circle of power and cursed, "And they have it protected."

"What kind of protection?" Lana asked.

"Looks like Runes and old magic." Randal nodded his head toward the talisman that was tucked under the table.

"What exactly does it protect from?" Ed asked from his post near the door.

I frowned examining the rune and the talisman as best I could, "It looks like life. From what I can see it's meant to stop anything that is alive from passing through it. But then how could they get to it?"

"No clue, but good for us that I, technically, am not alive." Lana grinned as she stepped up next to me. Rolling her neck she reached through the forcefield and grabbed the mirror. I held out the small dark purple velvet bag and she slipped it inside.

I tightened the strings on the bag and tucked it into the over padded jacket I wore. We slipped from the tent just as the lights from an incoming boat swept over us. I looked at the others. "Did someone else call for our ride?" I felt dread settle over me when they all shook their heads. We all turned towards the small dock where we had arrived and watched another boat pull up.

Chapter 24

I PUSHED KAT BEHIND me as Alec and Lana stepped to either side of me. Ed and Randal fanned out to either side of them, moving us into an arch around Kat. I watched as three women climbed out of the boat, each in a long coat that reminded me of the cloaks of old. They walked up the pier and stopped at the end facing us.

"What are you doing on our island?" The one in the middle asked, her head tilting to the side, voice high and squeaky.

"We came to reclaim what is ours by birth and to put a stop to the robbery you have been committing on the people surrounding this bay," I answered.

"Yours by birth?" The woman to the right asked, her voice a high-pitched whine, "You have all had more from birth than any one witch should be allowed. You have all become complacent in your over blessed life. We, the Forgotten Ones, have come to settle the score of our ancestors long ago."

"You all are nothing but treacherous cowards," hissed the third woman. Her voice was low and husky, "You come from lines who would sacrifice the less desirable to save their own skins."

"We don't know what you are talking about," Alec stated. "we are not the ones who killed innocents to steal from others."

The three women laughed and I felt the hair on my arms rise, "Innocents?" Spat the first woman again, "They were the children of murderers. You are the descendants of murderers. We seek vengeance."

"Step aside, let us leave and we will let you live," Randall said from next to Lana who had bared her fangs.

"It is not us who should worry about death. We are not the ones who have aligned ourselves with the murderous blood sucker," The third woman spat. Next to me Lana's fangs flashed in the moonlight as she hissed her displeasure.

"Now sisters," the second woman's voice whined out and it was like nails on a chalk board to my hears, "we should not taunt the blood sucker. She will soon learn what it is like to run in fear for her life."

"What do you mean?" Lana asked, her voice heavy with concern.

"Your people will soon know the pain of being hunted like the animals you are," cackled the second witch, "But don't worry dear. You will all last forever, truly immortal."

I could feel the wind picking up around us and shivered. I did not want to be on a boat in the middle of a storm, "let us leave," I ordered again and took a step towards the three women, "we do not wish to cause you any harm."

"But we wish to cause you harm," the third hissed, and below us it felt as if the earth quaked.

"Z, we have a problem," Kat said from behind me. Her voice was filled with a panicked fear, "There are animals clawing their way up from the ground, and they don't exactly look alive." I pulled out one of the explosion potions and threw it towards the three women hoping I would destroy the dock. They were raising freaking zombie animals.

"Oh you have got to be kidding me," I growled as Me and Kat stepped back to back, each of us arming ourselves with potion bottles. "Can you handle this Kat?" I asked softly as I watched a half decomposed brown bear claw its way up from the rocks.

"Don't have much of a choice," her voice didn't even hint at fear, "Let's kick their asses Z." I began to chuck potions at the animals as they pulled themselves from the earth. Around me others did the same. The entire Island flashes of color as the zombies were ignited with fire.

I whirled when I heard Kat give a short scream and found her on her back with a mangled wild cat of some kind on her. Before I could take a step toward her Randall's familiar Tyr had tackled the dead animal, knocking it off of her before he began to tear her apart. I ran over and offered a hand to lift her to her feet.

"You good?" I asked and was surprised when she grinned at me.

"This is the best thing I have ever done." She said through her heavy breathing, "When I get home, I'm telling Dad and Marilyn that I'm leaving and that I am one of the founders of AVEWS."

I grinned back at my twin and gave her a hard hug, "You are gonna rock this world sis."

"Damn right, now lets continue kicking their asses!" When she turned to run back into the fray I spotted one of the women moving toward the tend, glancing back over her shoulder repeatedly. I glanced over to check on the others and when they all seemed to be holding their own I took off at a light jog toward the creeping witch.

"What are you looking for?" I asked once I was within talking range. The witch jumped before whirling around to look at me. "If it's the mirror, I have to tell you its not in there anymore."

"Where is it?" Her voice was a growl. As she stepped toward me a low rumbling began over head just as the first drops of rain fell.

"No where you will ever get to it again."

"It is ours," she hollered, voice filling with rage as she stepped toward me.

"No, it was never yours. You killed to take things that were never yours, and you used them for self gain. Our powers were never meant to be used for gain." I had to yell the last words as the thunder turned to loud bangs and the rain pounded into the rocky ground. When she lunged at me I stumbled back words, feet slipping on the wet gravel. I fell as she wrapped her hands around my throat. Her body was heavy on my chest as she rode me to the ground, and before I had time to try to fight her off I was engulfed in cold water and I felt a sharp pain at the back of my head. *Alec*, it was the only thing I could think as everything went black and my lungs burned.

Chapter 25

I COULD FEEL MY heart pounding in my chest, explosions and screaming surrounded the air around me. I had been through this before and had to fight the flash backs that wanted to take over. The last time though the enemies were humans with guns and not witches with rabid zombie animals. Before the air was hot and dry, now I had to blink the rain from my eyes as a storm opened on us. As I threw one of the stunning potions at a mangled wolf, Croatoan leapt from next to me and took out a second canine as it jumped towards me. Her jaws locked around its throat. With a guttural growl and a vicious shake she separated the head from its body as she landed on the cold ground of the Island. Immediately she was back at my side and a sense of calm washed back over me. I reached down and rapped my hand into her fur, needing the calm, the reminder that we weren't back in the desert, but instead on a rock in the bay, despite the fact that again we were fighting for our lives. The touch calmed me, until my name whispered through my head. My head whipped around stopping when I saw Zander with one of the women riding his body to the ground. They were close to the waters lapped at the rocky shore, way to close. I didn't know if the crack I heard was of thunder or of Zanders head as I saw it bounce off something in the water in the flash of lightning. I ran towards them as fast as I could dogging through the mangled animal corpses around us, jumping over and around snapping jaws and slashing claws.

I pulled the witch off of Zander's now limp body and my heart ached. Without a second thought I gripped her head in both hands and twisted fast and hard till I heard her neck break, the sharp snap reverberating up my arms. I dropped her lifeless body to the ground without a thought and pulled Zander from the water, cradling him to my chest. His blue eyes staring up at me, and I could see the faint darkness of blood in the water. I dragged him to the more solid soil farther away from the water and laid him down.

"Breathe Damn it," I muttered linking my hands together before pushing hard over his heart, ignoring the sounds of the battle coming to an end behind me. Over and over again, I pushed until I heard bones snap in his chest. I pumped his heart, tears burning in my eyes, until every muscle in my arms went numb. Even as the gravel around him grew dark with blood that leaked from the back of his head, I continued the chest compressions, praying to every deity whose name came to my mind. I would give myself to all of them if they saved him here any now.

"Stop," I felt hands pulling at my shoulders and shoved them off. "Damn it Alec you have to stop." Randall pulled at my shoulders. Until I fell back away from Zander.

"I can save him," I screamed, voice desperate as I looked up at him. His eyes softened and he squeezed my shoulder.

"No you can't. I'm sorry but he's gone."

"Z?" Katia called limping her way over to us, her left arm held to her chest.

"I'm sorry," my voice choked as I moved over as she fell to her knees next to him, "I tried, I swear I tried." What was left of my heart shattered as she reached into Zander's soaked jacket and pulled out Dazzles limp form. The first sob slipped from my throat as Tyr howled into the night storm. Time seemed to stop around us as we grieved for another lost among us.

Chapter 26

Lana crawled up next to us and pulled a weeping Katia into her arms. I passed my hand over Zander's sea-drenched hair and I felt a fresh wave of tears wash over my face as I felt the small indent on the back of his head. Holding back my own sobs of grief I leaned down and pressed a kiss to his cold forehead before gently closing his blank staring eyes.

"The Mirror" Katia whispered from where she was cradled in Lana's arms, "Did they get the Mirror? We can't have let him die for nothing." I shook my head and ran my hands down his chest until I found the lump in his coat. Opening the soaked material I pulled the small disc from his pocket and had to fight not to throw it. This small disc was the reason I had lost him. Lana reached over, putting a supportive hand over my wrist and the world spun around me.

I was no longer kneeling on the wet gravely ground of the island but was standing in a stone courtyard. In front of me I could see an old Victorian house standing tall and proud in the moon light. Slowly I wandered through a stone gate as I gazed up at the old house. In the windows I could see statues, their stone faces twisted in pain and agony in flickering candle-light. I felt my pulse speed up and, as my gaze lowered from the windows, I noticed there were several of the same gruesome statues in the court-yard I had entered, filling the space between me and the house. Some were of two people intertwined, others were alone and curled in on them-selves. Still others had their heads tilt-ed back screaming to the sky. Care-fully I made my way to the closest statue. The woman it had been based on would have been beautiful; I could see that even though her face was twisted in pure agony. As I looked closer, I noticed the lengthened ca-nines in her snarling face. Vampire, I turned and rushed to another, this too was a vampire. As I spun to look at another the world swam around me again.

I fell to my hands and knees panting and shivering in the cool air of the island. "What did you see?" Katia asked, "you had a premonition when Lana touched you. They are very discombobulating the first time but I need you to think and fast, what did you see Alec?" her voice remained calm, as if she was used to coaching people through their first experience.

"A stone courtyard," I closed my eyes and thought back to the already fading vision, "A large Victorian style house, windows, lots of windows. There were people, no not people, statues in several of them. The statues were screaming. More statues in the courtyard with me. So much pain on their faces. Something different about their faces. Fangs, they had fangs, "I looked up at Lana, "the Vampires are in trouble, something is hurting them and turning them to stone."

"That's impossible" but her eyes flashed with fear.

"Go to the House of Ophiuchus, take people with you but go. Your people are in danger Lana." I didn't dare touch her again but I wanted to shove her toward the boat, to push her towards where she needed to go.

"We have to get off the Island First," Ed said. When I looked up I could see he was holding his right arm a little funny, "And I think we should all have Gwen look us over. Maybe get a tetanus or rabies shot."

"We can use the witches boat." Randall said. He looked at me, "Do you want me to help you carry Zander?" I felt a fresh wave of tears rush over my face but nodded. I handed the small mirror to Katia and gently tucked Dazzle under Zander's coat to keep them together. I pressed one last kiss to his forehead before I moved to stand at Zander's head while Randall moved to his feet. Together we lifted his body and moved him to the boat.

"We can't leave the Island like this," Ed said softly, "we can't chance anyone stumbling upon the monstrosities left here.

"What are we going to do?" Lana asked as she peered out over the acre of carnage.

"We still have some of the explosive potions. We put them around the Island," Katia said, her voice cold, "Once we are on the boat I can ignite them with a word."

We all nodded and dispersed across the Island, lining the shores with the small glass bottles. Once our pockets were empty we made our way into the boat the three sisters had ridden in on.

"I'll text the captain of the other boat and tell him that we don't need his services any longer," Katia said softly. The rough ride back to shore was silent. When we reached the dock I lifted Zander into my arms and carried him to the Van. I laid him in the far back, swallowing a fresh wave of tears as I closed the door. Ed wrapped a supportive arm around my shoulders and steered me into the front seat of the Van, as far from Zander's lifeless form as I could be. Crotoan jumped in and curled herself between my legs, her muzzle resting on my thigh. The drive to the Hotel was nearly as quiet as the boat ride to shore had been, the only sounds the girls soft sobs from the middle seat. We dropped the girls back at their vehicle and watched as they drove away, heading north before we began our own journey home.

Chapter 27

E D AND RANDAL TOOK turns driving back to New Orleans, leaving me in the front Passenger seat with Croatoan. The Familiars were all in the middle seat with who ever wasn't driving. Even with Croatoan pressed against my side the only thing I could feel was exhausted. We didn't stop this time, instead choosing to drive straight through. When we pulled up outside the house the others were all waiting outside for us.   "I need to go place the mirror on the Altar" I whispered the words. I wanted to believe what they were saying but I had lost too many friends in combat to hold out hope for Zander's return. I made my way up the stairs into the attic and crossed over the woven rug. I knelt in front of the Altar and gently laid the small mirror in the center of the etched design. As I did every gem in the worn wood glowed as did the Amethyst mirror, as if they were friends who were welcoming each other back.

When I opened the door Ade ran forward, "Where's Zander?" I just closed my eyes and shook my head. I couldn't bring myself to say the words even when I heard her soft sob. I pulled the younger girl into my arms as we both wept silently. When Eris came and took her from my arms, Randall and I moved around the back and carried Zander into the house. We brought him into the room where Kenna lay and set him on the small cot that had been placed next to the bed.

"They deserve better than a small bedroom" I said looking over at Gideon who had followed us in. I suddenly understood what he had been feeling for the last month, and didn't know how he was holding on as well as he was. All I wanted was to close my eyes and never open them again.

"Where else could we put them?"

"We will build them something in the back. Something made of glass so they can be warmed by the sun," Gwen said softly from the door, "When they awake, we can use it as a green house, but until then we can make it their sanctuary." I closed my eyes as grief washed over me in a fresh wave.

"Zander isn't like Kenna. He isn't in some kind of comma due to death in another realm, he is dead."

"If we can bring back Kenna, then we can bring back Zander," Gwen said firmly, "Gideon, you will need to wrap Zander in a time lock. Can you do that?"

Gideon nodded, "Yeah, I'll get started right away, and once the building is finished I can do the same thing, so that once inside time stops."

ACKNOWLEDGMENTS

There are so many people who have helped for this book. On top of those mentioned in the dedication at the beginning of this book I also want to thank my writers group. You guys have been an amzing resource and moral boost.

ABOUT AUTHOR

Ana Michelle was raised in Southeast-
ern Wisconsin, with two
younger siblings. Reading books was
the best way to get through the win-
ters
there. Ana started writing in the sixth
grade as her escape during summer
vacations. Since the first time she sat
down with a computer to type her
first
story, her aspiration was to be a
writer. Garnet Fire is her debut novel
and
the first book in the Gemstone Witch
Series.

www.ingramcontent.com/pod-product-compliance
Lightning Source LLC
Chambersburg PA
CBHW020143120726
47903CB00007B/2399